THE BAD BOY

THE FRIESSEN LEGACY

THE FRIESSENS
BOOK TWENTY-SIX

LORHAINNE ECKHART

Twitter: @LEckhart
Facebook: AuthorLorhainneEckhart

THE FRIESSEN FAMILY SERIES READING ORDER:

The Outsider Series

The Forgotten Child (Brad and Emily)
A Baby And A Wedding
Fallen Hero (Andy, Jed, and Diana)
The Search
The Awakening (Andy and Laura)
Secrets (Jed and Diana)
Runaway (Andy and Laura)
Overdue
The Unexpected Storm (Neil and Candy)
The Wedding (Neil and Candy)

The Friessens: A New Beginning

The Deadline (Andy and Laura)
The Price to Love (Neil and Candy)
A Different Kind of Love (Brad and Emily)
A Vow of Love, A Friessen Family Christmas

Long Past Dawn
How to Heal a Heart
Keep Me In Your Heart

The Friessen Family

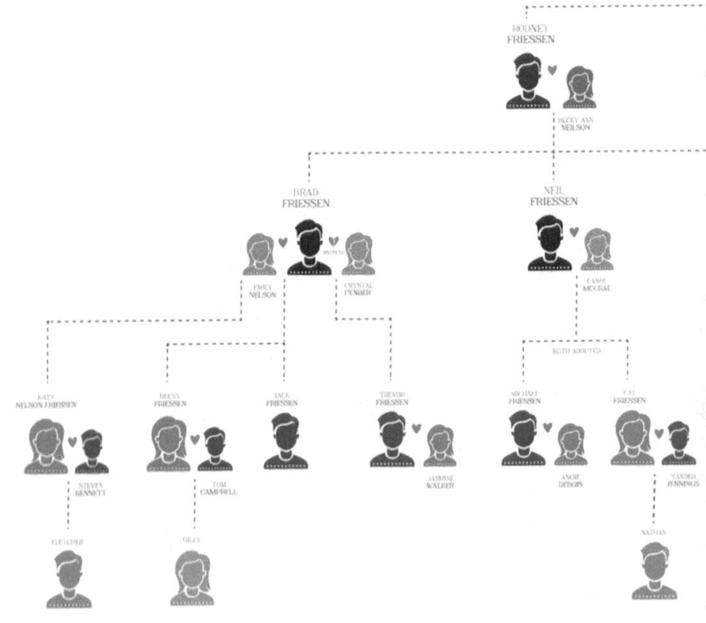

The Outsider Series

THE FORGOTTEN CHILD	BRAD & EMILY
A BABY AND A WEDDING	BRAD & EMILY & and 2nd 3rd babies & Becky
FALLEN HERO	JED, DIANA & ANDY
THE SEARCH	JED, DIANA & ANDY
THE AWAKENING	ANDY & LAURA

The Outsider Series

SECRETS	DIANA & JED with the entire Friessen Family
RUNAWAY	ANDY & LAURA
OVERDUE	JED & DIANA
THE UNEXPECTED STORM	NEIL & CANDY
THE WEDDING	NEIL & CANDY and the entire Friessen Family

The Friessens: A New Beginning

THE DEADLINE	ANDY & LAURA
THE PRICE TO LOVE	NEIL & CANDY
A DIFFERENT KIND OF LOVE	BRAD & EMILY
A VOW OF LOVE,	THE ENTIRE
A FRIESSEN FAMILY CHRISTMAS	FRIESSEN FAMILY

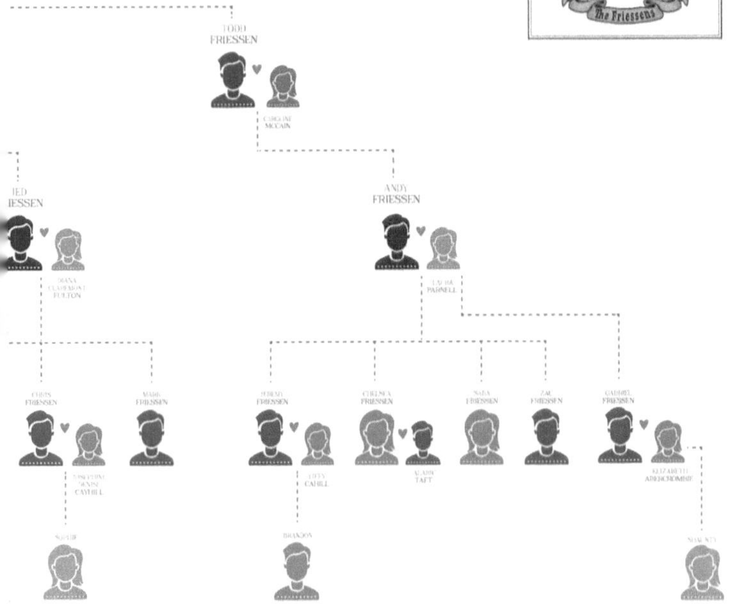

TODD FRIESSEN ♥ CAROLINE MCCAIN

JED FRIESSEN ♥ DIANA CLAIBORNE FULTON

ANDY FRIESSEN ♥ LAURA PARNELL

CHRIS FRIESSEN ♥ JOSEPHINE "JOSIE" CAYHILL

MARK FRIESSEN

SOPHIE

JEREMY FRIESSEN ♥ TIFFY CAHILL

CHELSEA FRIESSEN ♥ ALARIC TAFT

NADA FRIESSEN

ZAC FRIESSEN

GABRIEL FRIESSEN ♥ ELIZABETH ABERCROMBIE

BRAXTON

SHAUNEY

As the youngest brother, Mark Friessen refuses to answer to anyone. He's been called a restless bad boy because responsibility for his father's ranch has never rested on his shoulders, even though he loves everything about the life of a cowboy. Working with the horses and the land, being in charge, and doing all the hard work on the ranch has always settled his restless nature—that is, until a rodeo queen broke his heart by running off with his best friend after two-timing him for six long months.

The funny thing about broken hearts is that they make people do things they wouldn't do if they were thinking clearly, as his mother so succinctly advised him during his ensuing dating spree. This is likely why Mark has now signed up to be a deputy in the next county over, with a badge, a gun, and the kind of power he thought he wanted.

When he pulls mousy young librarian Daria McKenzie over for speeding, she is speechless and furious when she realizes he doesn't remember who she is. This bad boy has left a trail of broken hearts in his wake—including hers.

ONE

Mark Friessen knew heads turned every time he stepped into the Main Street Café in North Lakewood—namely the heads of all the women. Married, single, didn't matter. But not everyone looked at him fondly.

No, he was well aware he'd left a string of broken hearts behind him, all because of one Cindy Grant. Short, curvy, and flirtatious, Cindy had a generous bust, the most gorgeous long, wavy dark hair, eyes the color of taffy, a smile to die for, and a personality that would've made him do anything for her. He'd been proud to say she was his girlfriend until he'd figured out what everyone else already knew. His best friend, Randy Meyer, had been screwing her for the entire six months Mark had dated her.

His body, mind, and soul still zeroed in on her where she was cozied up to Randy in a booth, sharing a plate of fries. Just seeing them together could still pack a miserable sucker punch right in his stomach that left him with that uneasy sick feeling. At the same time, he knew he was his own worst enemy because he couldn't look away. He let his gaze linger, staring, when he needed to get over it. But how could he get past a knife shoved in his back by two people he'd trusted?

He rested his hand on his duty belt, feeling the weight of the pistol, the cuffs. For a second, he took some measure of pride in the power he was carrying, his badge, his gun, and the importance he now had. But his gaze lingered a little too long again, and he had to force himself to look away, taking in the familiar faces staring up at him.

He took a seat at one of the three empty stools at the counter and reached for a laminated menu, but he could still hear Cindy's soft laugh. His fingers curled involuntarily around the menu as he pictured his hand wrapping around her neck and squeezing all that soft skin he had tasted. He couldn't pull the want of her from his head. Just thinking of her, hearing her, feeling her in the room had him feeling like a lovesick puppy. What the hell was wrong with him?

He realized that Betty Hargrave, a long-time friend of his mother's, was standing in front of him with a pad, ready to take his order. She was his mom's age, in a white blouse and black pants, likely more than fifty pounds over-weight. "Ignore them," she said. "Don't you know that letting them see they're getting to you means they've won? You're made of stronger stuff, Mark. Get her out of your head and move on. She didn't deserve you, and you have more important things to focus on, like your new job. By the way, congrats. Heard you were picked up as a deputy in the county over. Your mother is so proud..." Betty glanced over his head and stopped talking.

Mark pulled off his cowboy hat, ran his fingers through his thick red hair, and rested it on the counter beside him. He fixed Betty with what he hoped was his newly mastered cop gaze.

She didn't seem impressed. "I'm just saying it's time

you move on in more productive, healthier ways. You're not fooling anyone with the way you walked in here and zeroed in on her, staring them both down with that hurt puppy look you're doing a piss-poor job of hiding. I'm just glad you didn't hike on over to their table and start some trouble."

There was nothing worse than having his broken heart shoved in his face. "Not sure what you're talking about," he said. "I've moved on. Got a great job, an important job, in law enforcement. I'm not the one who starts trouble, but I sure as shit will shut it down." He glanced back to the menu, not seeing the items he knew by heart. "I'll take a big order of fried chicken to go. Actually, make it a double order of the whole chicken, and add in three family packs of fries and coleslaw. Told my mom I'd pick up dinner on my way home." He tucked the menu back in the slot, taking in the case of pies on display and the open window through which he could see the cook in back. "And toss in a blueberry pie, the whole pie." He flicked his hand to the pie case.

"You're not fooling me, Mark," Betty said. "Can still see how torn up you are. That kind of road rash is all thick and crusty, and you can't hide it. They're married. Let it go. It's been how long now? You've got to forget about her and Randy." She was scribbling his order on paper and ripped it from the pad. "Order up," she said, shoving the paper on a metal swivel with all the others before reaching for a mug and setting it in front of him to pour him a coffee even though he hadn't asked for one. That was something everyone did, thinking coffee made everything better.

"It wasn't your best friend who was messing with your girl," he snapped, his back burning as if Cindy and Randy had figured out he was there. He hated that feeling. He hated, too, the fact that everyone knew what a fool he'd been.

Betty rested the carafe of coffee on the counter and cocked her hip, staring at him with the same look his mother did when she wanted to talk some sense into him. He wished she'd stop talking about it, stop bringing it up.

"Nope," she said. "It was a shitty thing that happened, and it wasn't just your friend; it was her, too. Just the same, Mark, you're not all squeaky clean, either. How many of the local girls have you dated to, as you said, get her out of your system? I have to say, I counted a different girl on your arm every few days. What was it, a palate cleanser, as you so aptly put it? You likely left every one of those girls with a broken heart. You treated them as if they were nothing. Consider the heartache you have right now. Those girls are likely wondering what the hell they did."

He squeezed his mug, thinking of the women he'd gone through. This was the first time someone other than his mom had pointed out to him how wrong he was. All the women's faces and names were starting to blend one into the next, which was not good, but he wasn't about to admit to anyone what a prick he'd been. His face heated. Damn, why was it taking so long for them to cook that chicken?

"Don't want to answer? That's okay," Betty said. "Your expression says it all. Let me point out to you, since I'm already on a roll and since you're going to have to wait for your order, that when you're as damn attractive as you are—and you are hot, just like your father and your older brothers—women want you. But you playing the field the way you have and tossing them away like garbage makes you no better than the one you're still pining for. Those girls had feelings, real feelings, and having a broken heart ain't no excuse for doing what you've done. So before you continue on with another girl in the hopes of getting Cindy out of your mind, try to give the girls you take out the same consideration you wanted from her. Get your head straight, take some time alone, and stop the age-old art men have of moving on to another woman just because they're afraid of being alone."

He rested his coffee on the counter and felt a hand on his shoulder.

"Hey, Mark, heard you got a job with the sheriff's department in the next county over?" It was Carl Sullivan, a friend of his dad's, in red plaid and baggy jeans. He had a grizzled look, with his graying hair and mustache in need of a trim. Mark hoped to hell he hadn't heard his dressing-down.

"I did," Mark said. "Started this week." He had to fight the urge to point out the obvious badge pinned to his shirt and the holstered gun, and he wondered what Carl's amused expression meant.

"Well, great to see you," Carl said. "Say hi to your parents for me." Then he left just as Mark heard his order being called and turned back to see Betty bagging up the food.

He pulled his wallet from his pocket, downed another swallow of the bitter coffee, and pulled some cash out to toss on the counter.

"Oh, hey there, Mark. Didn't see you sitting here. How're you doing?"

What was it about her voice? She still had the ability to bring him to his knees. Betty glanced behind him with horror, and he turned to see Cindy. Randy towered over her, resting a possessive hand on her shoulder. He'd been a friend once, Mark's best friend, but now he was someone whose face he would just as soon have planted his fist in.

Apparently, Randy had the same idea, by the way he stared back at him. Hate was hate.

"Cindy, Randy," he bit out, standing up and resting his hand beside the butt of his gun. He pulled in a breath, knowing his former friend had little to offer in return. He knew Randy saw the badge pinned to the chest of his light brown deputy's uniform, and he silently wished he'd do something he could use to justify taking him down and cuffing him.

"You joined the sheriff's department? That's fantastic," Cindy said. "I've thought so much about you and hoped you were doing okay. Was just telling Randy that I haven't seen you around much as of late. Now I see why. Wow, had no idea you were going into law enforcement. Thought you had your eye on running your dad's place."

He'd forgotten how much he'd shared with Cindy, and now he wished he hadn't. It was the kind of personal information he shared only with someone he could trust. What was it about hindsight? "Oh, you know, there's something fulfilling about being a cop and seeing to it that folks stay law-abiding." He heard a throat clear behind him and turned back to Betty.

"Here's your change, Mark," she said. "By the way, nice of you to buy dinner for your family. It's warm, so you'd best get moving so it's not cold by the time you get home. Again, say hi to your mom and dad for me."

He waved off the change and pocketed his wallet, not missing the warning in Betty's blue eyes, a warning he should heed if he were smart. "Will do," he said, then lifted his cowboy hat to his head.

Cindy and Randy were still there. He pasted a tight smile to his face, and Cindy returned it brightly and shrugged. Randy was still giving him a look that told him to eat shit and die, and it was damn awkward.

"Well, hope to see you around a lot more, Mark. Take care of yourself, you hear?" She actually touched his arm, and his eyes zeroed right in on her hand, taking in the flash of diamond, another reminder she belonged to another man. Then she lifted her fingers in a wave, and she and Randy were out the door. He swore under his breath and started after them.

"Mark," Betty called out, and he turned back. "You forget something?"

"Right." He took in the two paper bags stuffed with dinner and dessert which he planned to take back to his parents, Chris, JD, Danny, Evie, and the girls, and he felt that sense of idiocy wash over him again.

"Again, I can't stress it enough: Leave it be," Betty said. "You're not friends, you'll never be friends, and the way you and Randy are circling one another, I'd just as soon not have a fight started in my diner."

He lifted the bags, and for a second he wanted to protest that it had been Cindy and Randy who approached him, not the other way around. But he said none of that in the face of the warning staring back at him.

"Fine," he said, then started to the door, juggling the bags.

He pulled it open and made his way to his silver Mustang, where he rested the bags on top of the car and pulled out his keys. Cindy and Randy were across the road at his pickup, his tongue down her throat and his hands on her ass. Instead of looking away, he just watched them until Randy was suddenly looking his way.

Yeah, what an asshole. Mark swore one day soon, he'd settle things with Randy, and that one thought brought a smile to his lips. It would be a day of reckoning for the knife in his back. It was only a matter of time.

"You and me, Randy. Payback is coming," Mark said

under his breath, then forced himself to look away as he pulled open the door to the car he'd bought because the girl his best friend had stolen had wanted him to buy it. As Mark tucked the bags in the back seat and slid behind the wheel, Randy pulled out with his window down and, as he drove past, lifted his middle finger.

TWO

"Hey there, Uncle Mark," said his niece Ally, who was looking more and more like her mom every day. Her lower two front teeth were missing, and she had the same brilliant red hair that had been passed from Diana to each of her sons, Chris, Danny, and Mark.

Ally slid onto the stool at the island of the open-concept kitchen. His parents had finally bitten the bullet and renovated, knocking out the wall and putting in two wall ovens and high-end appliances—likely because they all still lived under one roof at their ranch. JD, his sister-in-law, was the one who did all the cooking. Mark took in his niece and realized having a minute alone was something that would never happen there.

"So how was work today, kid?" Mark asked as he slid a plate to her, half expecting Sophie, his other niece, Danny and Evie's daughter, to come running in next.

"I'm in grade four, Uncle Mark. I'm too young to work. And do you know what the best part of school is?"

She was so darn cute. He wasn't the kind of guy who was partial to kids, but in his mind, his two nieces were perfect.

"Let me guess, recess?"

She actually rolled her eyes, and he had to fight the urge to laugh. "No, the bus, silly! I got old Mrs. Kruger, and she's always cranky. Today she yelled at us, saying we were a bunch of misbehaving, inconsiderate misfits, and if we didn't smarten up, she was going to make us all stay in and miss recess for a week. We weren't doing nothing wrong. She just wanted us to sit quietly and not move. Do you know how hard that is?" The spark in her bold blue eyes was so innocent and trusting, and he didn't want any adult to take that away from her.

"Did you tell your mom and dad?" he asked.

She shrugged and shook her head. "Nope, just you. Remember you told me how women complain a lot? Well, I know I wasn't supposed to be listening, but I heard her talking with another teacher at recess, and she had a fight with her husband. Apparently, he keeps leaving the toilet seat up and leaves everything in the house a mess for her to clean. She's not very nice sometimes. I thought about telling her that if she came to our house, she'd see that the toilet seat is always up here and that my mom is always cleaning up after my dad and you, but she doesn't complain."

Of course, he laughed. She was so cute and direct, but damn, had he really done that to JD? "Well, I can do my part," he said. "I didn't realize I was just walking out and leaving things. Habit, I guess. I'll make sure to pick up after myself so your mom isn't having to do it."

Ally reached for a chicken leg from one of the two boxes he'd opened and set on the island. "I'm sure my mom would appreciate it," she said as she took a bite, for a moment sounding so mature.

"So you're in charge of dinner?" Chris said as he strode in, his red hair long and tied back. He grabbed a plate. Mark hadn't known his brother was home.

"Figured I could do my part," he said again. "Where is everyone?"

Chris stuck his hand in the box of fries and dumped half on his plate along with two breasts. "Dad's in the barn, and Mom and Danny are back in the office. Hey, squirt, eat up," he said as he tousled Ally's hair. Then he walked out the door to the barn.

Mark knew their dad's life revolved around this ranch, the horses. He felt envy for a moment because it had been the only thing he'd ever wanted to do. He knew Chris didn't have the same passion for this place that he did, but there they were. He stared at the door Chris had just walked through, then back to his niece, who, he had to remind himself, was only ten and not his confidante.

"But your teacher sounds like a problem," Mark said. "I remember having trouble with a few in school myself, but then, I wasn't that easy. Sitting still wasn't something I was about to do, either. You want me to go and have a talk with her? I'll flash my badge and show her who's in charge, and I'll tell her if she doesn't behave and treat you nicely, I'll be coming back—and that's something she doesn't want." Mark scooped some of the salad onto Ally's plate and some onto his as he listened to her giggle.

"Oh, Uncle Mark, no, you can't do that. It's fine."

"Why not? Of course I can. It says right here I can." He tapped a finger to the deputy's badge pinned to his chest, but she just rolled her eyes. "Okay, but if you change your mind, just say the word and I'm there. Better still, why don't I take you into school this week, and I can have a friendly talk with her?"

She actually reached over and rested her hand on his,

and her gaze dropped to his gun, still holstered. "Uncle Mark, you just want to scare her, is all. Maybe you could just tell her what Grandma says to all of us, to leave her problems at home and not take it out on everyone, because we are, after all, just kids."

Great advice. He heard Danny now in the office with his mom at the back of the house, likely talking over some big case, but he didn't have a clue where JD and Evie were. Chris hadn't elaborated, but then, his brother wasn't known for talking.

"So where's your mom?" Mark said, taking in all the food and the plates he'd stacked. He'd expected a convergence on the food as soon as he walked in.

Ally took a huge bite of chicken and looked up at him. "She's in town with Aunt Evie and Sophie. Sophie's dance recital is today."

He took in his niece, who wore faded blue jeans and kid-size cowboy boots that she never seemed to take off unless she was sleeping or bathing. Add in her long, soft reddish hair, which seemed to go every which way, and her innocent clear blue eyes, and of course she had a corner of his heart. He would do anything for her. "So how come you're not there too?" he said. "You should be dancing. You and Sophie do everything together." They were practically twins, even though they were cousins, Sophie being Danny and Evie's, Ally being Chris and JD's. Ally was all tomboy and horses, whereas Sophie was Barbie dolls and dresses.

She made a face. "That's not my thing. I like horses and playing in the barn and getting dirty, as my mom puts it. Sophie likes to dance and play dress-up. I don't have time for such things, and I sure didn't want to sit and watch a bunch of whining and crying from girls who can barely dance. Do you have any idea how boring that is?"

He had to fight the urge to laugh.

Just then, Danny walked into the kitchen, wearing blue jeans, a white T-shirt, and a two-day beard, his red hair cut short. Their mom, Diana, was behind him, her deep red hair lighter from the gray that had crept in. She wore a blue tracksuit, still slim, and she stepped behind Ally, swept her arms around her, and kissed her cheek over and over. Ally giggled. He knew his mom couldn't get enough of her granddaughters and the mayhem of them all living under her roof.

"Mark, see you got dinner. Thank you. So how was deputy duty?" Danny remarked as he grabbed a plate and rummaged through the pieces. Mark knew he was looking for something big, with substance. He pulled out two thighs and dug into the coleslaw. There was something off about the way his brother spoke to him, though. Mark couldn't shake the feeling that he wasn't being taken seriously.

"It was great. What can I say? It's the perfect job. Get to carry a gun, a badge. Kind of forces people to respect you, to behave, mind their Ps and Qs. I love it."

His mom stilled, and her eyes widened—in shock or dismay, he wasn't sure. The hard look Danny leveled him with was that of a big brother about to lecture him or bring him down a few notches. Mark wished he could go back a couple of seconds and not say what he just had. He couldn't help that his personal feelings had taken free rein again.

"That kind of thinking can land you in a world of trouble, little brother," Danny said. "It's definitely been the downfall of a number of cops. Word of advice, Mark? Don't be one of them."

Diana raised a brow but said nothing, and he could feel Ally staring up at him, her eyes wide. He didn't like the scrutiny, so he bit into a piece of chicken. His mom had busied herself with dishing up some slaw and fries, and she rummaged in the second box before picking out a wing.

"Now, Danny," she started, "you, Chris, and Mark are all the same in that one respect: You push it with everything. Mark, as I've told you before, sometimes when someone has hurt you, you do things you wouldn't do if you were thinking clearly. Your dad and I didn't say anything when you took this job even though you've never given us the slightest clue that you were interested in law enforcement, in being on the front lines. Just be sure you understand that having a badge doesn't give you the right to hold it over anyone or go on a power trip, so to speak. You be respectful, because being a cop is supposed to mean looking after the rights of the little guy, not kicking ass because someone has pissed you off. At the same time, and I'm just going to say it because it's time, I wonder if this is a reaction to what happened with Cindy."

Mark could feel Ally still staring up at him. He felt very much as if his mom were ready to pick up where Betty had left off not even an hour earlier. He was so done with talk of a girl he would've done anything for, had done everything for, before she kicked him to the curb.

"I am respectful," he said. "I'm also the law. This has nothing to do with her. I'm over her. Like, seriously, Mom…"

"Well, just a minute now." Diana didn't let him finish. "Betty called and said you ran into Cindy and Randy at the diner."

Danny lifted a brow, watching him with the steady gaze he'd mastered, which he used when he was trying to set someone straight or tell Mark how he should be thinking or feeling.

"You know, Mark, you need to move on," Diana said. "They're married, and we've had this talk. She chose him.

You have to reconcile all of that hurt I can see you're still carrying. Let it go, move on, because they have a life together now—and I heard they're expecting, too."

That was the one thing he hadn't wanted to hear. Obviously, his mom realized, by the way her expression softened. He needed to roll his shoulders because of the tension that pulled across them. He felt sucker punched, and it had to be written all over his face.

"Oh, Mark, you didn't know?"

What was he supposed to say? He'd run into the girl who still had his heart tangled up in knots, and now she was pregnant with his best friend's kid? It was over, and he'd known that before. She'd moved on and was married, but now that ultimate commitment, a baby, killed the hope he'd never have admitted was still there. He dropped his piece of chicken on his plate and had to fight the urge to roll his shoulders again, his appetite gone. "Seriously, Mom, you think I want this rubbed in my face? How about you let it go," he said, then realized it had come out rather sharply.

Diana said nothing, just glanced once to Danny.

"It's okay, Uncle Mark," Ally said. "She's not good enough for you. You need to forget her. You have me and Sophie."

Damn, he loved that kid. He found it easier to look down into the innocence that stared up at him with wise eyes, so serious. "Thanks, Ally. Don't worry, she's forgotten. Just need everyone to stop bringing her up. I got you and Soph. That's all I need." He nudged her.

His mom lifted her eyes to the ceiling, and Danny was just shaking his head as if he too had more to say. But Mark wasn't interested in another lecture about what he should be doing.

"Hey, again," he continued, "one good thing in my life

is the fact that I have the perfect job, which I love. I mean, who wouldn't want to be a deputy? I get a badge, a gun. What more is there to want? I get to pull over dick-heads…" He stopped, taking in the look leveled his way by his mom, Danny, and Ally. "Oops, sorry. I mean bad people."

He took in the exchange between his mom and Danny just as the front door opened and his dad stepped in. Of course, his dad zeroed right in on the gun he still had holstered to his side.

"Make sure you discharge that," Jed said, "and be doubly sure it's not loaded. Lock that up when you're home. I don't want to ever find that lying around with the girls. Gun safety, Mark."

There it was, his dad treating him as if he didn't know any better. After all, he was the cop, not his dad.

"Always do," he said, thinking of the gun safe on the top shelf of his closet, which his dad had insisted on since day one of his new job. Damn, why did his dad still go straight to treating him like a wet-behind-the-ears kid?

"And that brings me to something else I wanted to mention," Mark said. "Your timing is great, Dad, since I'll have to say this only once."

His dad lingered by his mom, who had handed him a plate.

"I'm moving out," Mark said. "Looking for a place over in Clancy, close to work." It would give him the space he needed without one more person asking him if he knew what he was doing or treating him as if he were still a kid.

"You sure about that, son? Mighty expensive. And this is home, you know that."

Yeah, an overcrowded home, with Chris and Danny both there with their wives and his nieces. He loved them all, but sometimes he just needed to make a fresh start.

"Time to leave the nest, Dad. Besides, you have Chris and Danny. You don't need me hanging around, too."

Their expressions were full of shock, as if they couldn't believe what he'd just said. Except he'd meant every bit of it. Danny had his place there, and Chris had his as well, but Mark was the last born, and as he looked around at what was left, he realized he needed to make his own way.

CHAPTER

THREE

His windows were rolled down in the sheriff's cruiser as he listened to the buzz over the scanner, parked on a side road outside Mount Vernon, where he was assigned to traffic duty. Of all the jobs, he'd never expected this one, which, as far as he was concerned, was a total waste of his time and talent.

Apparently, as had been pointed out to him again that morning by Sheriff Prescott, a big man with a deep voice, a scowl, and a personality one didn't argue with, this was the lifeblood of the sheriff's office and the revenue needed to keep it flowing, and the new guy wasn't needed anywhere but parked out there, bored out of his mind. It gave him too much time to think about things he didn't want to be thinking about, namely Cindy.

What was it about her? He still couldn't get her out of his mind. It wasn't as if she was a supermodel; she was short, with a slight overbite and a plump butt he loved to sink his hands into. He still wanted her, which only made him angry, because as much as he told himself to, he couldn't hate her. Instead, his first thought was always of her smile and the way he hadn't been able to keep himself from touching her, reaching out to her like a drug that his body, mind, and soul couldn't break free of.

Not one woman he'd taken out and slept with had excited him the way Cindy could. He let out a heavy sigh and pulled his hand over his face just as his radar beeped, and he jumped, seeing the flash of a green Sunfire whipping past. His heartbeat kicked up as he started his car and pulled out, flooring it, flicking on his sirens as he chased down the speeding compact, putting everything he could into pulling over that dirtbag.

This was the only thrill he'd had in what felt like hours of boredom. The car signaled, slowed, and pulled over, and he parked behind it, boxing it in. Then he called in to dispatch, radioing the license plate number.

He stepped out of his car, the lights still flashing but the siren now silent, and took in the idling Sunfire, taking his time to notice anything that seemed off. A glance in the back told him there was just the one driver.

He stopped at the window and tapped on the glass as he took in the woman behind the wheel, seeing no one else. She rolled her window down, revealing shoulder-length brown hair, dark-rimmed glasses, and full pink lips.

"Any idea how fast you were going there, ma'am?" He looked down into the back seat, the passenger side, noting a black purse on the seat but nothing else from where he stood. His hand rested on the top of the car, the other close to the butt of his gun.

"Not a clue. You're going to tell me I was speeding, right? Well, so be it. Give me the damn ticket. I'm late for work."

He took in the young woman staring up at him, her blue eyes lit with a fire he hadn't expected. He wondered if she had any idea that was exactly what she shouldn't do with a cop. He pulled his shades down a bit and stared over the rims at her, a motion he knew intimidated many. She just glared back with all the annoyance it appeared she could muster.

"Okay, you want to play it this way? License and registration," he snapped, and he watched the hesitation and then the shake of her head, the huff of annoyance under her breath. Seriously, this lady was pushing her luck. She reached into the glovebox for her registration and then into her wallet for her license and handed them to him rather forcefully, still unexpectedly pissed off. He took in the name Daria McKenzie.

"Do you mind stepping out of the car?" he said rather sharply and stepped back, taking in her shock.

"Are you serious?" she snapped again, ready to tear a strip off his ass. "Wow, you really are a piece of work."

What the hell? He stepped back as she got out of the car, taking in her long legs, the skirt that stopped at her knees, and the high collar of her sleeveless shirt, ultra conservative. She was maybe five foot five, cute, slender. Neat and tidy and not a stitch of makeup on.

"Let's get something straight, miss," he said. "I have no time for this attitude of yours, and right now, I have you at thirty over the limit, which is bordering on reckless driving. You want to tell me why you were in such a hurry?" He allowed his gaze to linger and wished he had a piece of gum he could work.

"Miss?" She leaned in a bit, tense. She really had gone straight to a fight response instead of doing what most women did, batting her lashes, flicking him a smile, and playing dumb, trying to charm her way out of a ticket. "So that's what I'm reduced to, seriously? Guess I should have known, but never expected you were a cop. Not in a million fucking years! So you have me on speeding, reckless driving? I think not, Mark! It is Mark, right?" She was direct, and he sensed the challenge. It seemed she knew him. She didn't pull that gaze from him. All he could do was stare, trying to place her, racking his brain, trying to figure it out.

"I'm confused," he said. "Have we met? The name's Deputy Mark Friessen."

She stiffened and fisted her hands, flicking those fired-up blue eyes to him. Her mouth tightened, and she shook her head with an angry toss, the same one he'd seen both his sisters-in-law pull on his brothers. There was just something about an angry woman. He could always tell when one believed he'd crossed that magical line he was supposed to know existed.

"You seriously don't remember?" she said. "Guess I should've known, considering you called me honey the whole time. Stupid me, I thought it was a nickname or some term of endearment. I figured it was just something you liked to call a woman. Evidently, remembering my name wasn't important." She pulled her arms across her chest and actually rolled her eyes, and for a second, his chest tightened as he again tried to place her. Alarm bells went off in his head as he reminded himself to breathe.

"I can tell by the look on your face that you're still trying to figure out where you know me from, and it's not coming to you," she said. "It's eluding you, that mystery. You know what? I should be hurt, but frankly, I'm on the other side already, kind of pissed off to know I'm so…forgettable."

He didn't know what to say. He took in the woman, willing a memory to return, some hint, before he jammed his other foot in his mouth. She must have known, as she lifted her brows as if expecting him to say something.

"Uh…" he started. Damn, he was at a loss for words.

She lifted the flat of her hand to stop him. "Seriously, save your dignity. You don't remember me. For me, it should be a crushing blow, but thankfully, I like myself enough that I refuse to let it bring me down. Yes, Deputy Mark Friessen, you're all that, hot stuff, eye candy…" She actually flitted her hand in the air, gesturing his way as if making a point. "But that's all you are. Should've known, with how the night started out. Not even dinner, just freebie happy-hour appies, because you weren't trying to impress me. You had a couple wings, downed a beer, talked nonstop about yourself. Let me remind you, you were the one who came over to where I was, minding my own business, having a glass of wine. Of course, I realize the interest was all one-sided. Can't figure out why you bothered. It was just about a one-night stand, just S-E-X…" She actually spelled it out.

He wondered if his face paled. Not good. Why couldn't he remember who she was, remember that night? He needed a clue. The bar had to be the Horned Toad, which was pretty much the only one he frequented for a pint, free appies, and women. Right, all so he could forget Cindy.

"Well, this is awkward," he said. "I see you're angry over it. I guess I should apologize, then, for…"

She lifted her hand again and actually shut her eyes. He wasn't sure whether the sound she made was a laugh or a snort, but he was sure it signified disgust, anger. He knew well when a woman didn't want to hear his excuses or what he had to say, so he shut up. He'd seen his mom and his two sisters-in-law often enough with Danny, Chris, and his dad.

"Hey, no biggie," she said. "You picked me up against my better judgement, which was prodding me to tell you to get lost. I thought you were cute, an attractive hottie, and I had a moment of weakness and ignored the warning that you might be just man candy, nothing of substance. We had a few drinks, you said all the right things, and you talked me into driving out to Millers Landing, by the pond, even though we'd just met. Then you kissed me and talked me into the back seat of your Mustang, and then it was over. Wham, bam, so fast. It became clear you didn't care about satisfying me. It was all about you and your needs and an overcrowded back seat.

"Then you drove me back, dropped me off, and didn't even have the courtesy to get out of your car and walk me to mine. You stayed behind the wheel with a 'See ya, honey,' not even a kiss, then drove away while I was still standing there. So the fact that you're now pulling me over and can't remember who I am is pathetic, really, for you." She actually reached over and jabbed her finger into his chest.

He squeezed the license and registration and handed them back to her. For a second, all she did was stare up at him. Then she glanced to the papers and took them back.

"I'm sorry," he said. It was all he could think to say, knowing it likely didn't come close to making right what he'd done—which he vaguely remembered now, even though her face at the time had blended into all the other faceless women he'd screwed in a desperate need to get Cindy out of him. Only now did he have the first inkling that maybe what he'd done wasn't okay. No, it definitely wasn't okay.

"So, my ticket?" she prompted, gesturing to him. The lack of emotion in her voice did little to hide how pissed off she still was.

He just shook his head and lifted his hands. "I'll let you off with a warning, Daria. And again, you aren't forgettable." He was about to flash her a smile, but the way she stared up at him told him to go to hell, and he realized she'd likely help him there if he was having trouble finding the way. Damn, this really wasn't going well.

"Please spare me that sweet-talk bullshit," she said. "I've already had the experience with you, and it wasn't anything memorable. Just so you know, all you have going on wasn't as great as I expected. So thank you for letting me off with a warning, but it definitely wasn't a pleasure. Now can I go and get back in my car? Because I'm late for work, and spending one more minute with you is exactly what I don't want to do."

He didn't miss the unveiled anger in her tone, the spirit, the fight, the fact that she'd just said *Fuck you* without actually saying the words. So what did he do but reach for her license and registration and rip them from her hands?

"On second thought, let me go write your ticket up. Now, don't go anywhere," he said, leaning in, though he knew he should just let her go.

Her mouth opened and her eyes widened as if he'd just yanked the rug out from under her. This one-upmanship wasn't showing him in a flattering light, considering what he'd done, but there was something he couldn't stand about anyone daring to challenge him or call him out.

He walked back to his cruiser, pulled open the door, and slid inside, taking in the woman, one of many with whom he'd had a one-night stand. She turned to her car, her hands fisted, and he thought she swore before kicking her tire.

Yeah, she was pissed, hot under the collar, and not what he'd expected. He read her name again from the license with the mugshot photo and wondered, how in the world had he ever forgotten about Daria McKenzie?

FOUR

Saturdays were the kind of freakishly busy days that brought out all sorts to the library, from people with stupid questions, to unruly kids dragged by short-tempered mothers or distracted fathers, to teens hanging out, to busy nine-to-fivers stocking up on their weekly reads. It was a steady hum in a library that was supposed to be quiet.

Daria stacked the last of the returned books onto the cart after running them through the scanner, listening to the familiar creaks of the library, one of the oldest buildings in North Lakewood. This was the one day of the week she wished she didn't work. Her feet were aching, but the day was almost over, and she was counting the minutes until five o'clock because she was ready to head home.

"Daria, can you lock up in about five minutes?" said Carol Hodges, the head librarian, with a wave of her hand as she strode around the counter. "I just told the kids hanging in back to pack it up and head on out. I think everyone else is gone, though. You may as well leave those books until the morning, you know, put them away then."

She was a motherly boss, with short gray hair, married to the mayor, and she'd always given Daria a friendly ear when she needed it. She was suited to dealing with chaos and unruliness with patience and a firmness no one dared to cross.

"You know what? I'll stay a bit after I lock up to make up for the time I was late this morning," Daria said. Just then, she heard the ding of the door, and wham, there it was, the annoyance at some inconsiderate jerk who was pushing it by coming in this late. "We're closing in five minutes," she called out, and Carol lifted a brow, likely because of how sharply she'd said it. "What?"

Carol shook her head. "Remember, be nice. We're here to serve the public, you know, to encourage a love of books."

Daria heard footsteps, the creak of the floor, and felt anger first of all as she took in Mark Friessen in his deputy's uniform, lifting his hat off his head and running his fingers through that thick red neatly cut hair. His shades were tucked into his shirtfront, and he was walking her way.

"Ladies," he said with a nod to Carol and then her.

Of course, her stomach bottomed out. She took in his swagger, all that frickin' man candy, tall and broad shouldered. Being that good looking seemed so wrong. Worse, she wondered whether she'd ever get the feel of his hands touching her out of her mind. Nope, it was burned there forever, and just seeing him now, looking her way, she still felt the heat that had been responsible for her moment of bad judgement.

"As I said, we're closing in five minutes." She lifted her wrist, taking in her watch. "Actually, make that three." She knew her voice was cool, and she had held up her fingers to make a point. Carol stared at her, obviously taken aback by her tone, with a little amusement, she thought, at her expense.

Mark, though, flashed her that super-flirty sexy smile she supposed he was born with, the one she knew well had once made her so willing to do anything for him. Damn him, anyway. She hoped she was smarter now.

He let out a soft laugh under his breath, and she knew he wasn't impressed. "Well, I'll make this quick, then. It's about earlier today. I wanted to have a word with you, because how we left it didn't sit right with me."

Carol was looking from him to her, and Daria felt her interest. She forced herself to drag her gaze from Mark as she struggled not to roll her shoulders under Carol's scrutiny or explain their history.

"The reason I was late," she said. "I was speeding, and this deputy pulled me over. He then insisted on dragging me out of my car to treat me like a common criminal and took extra time writing up a ticket. So now you're here to, what, add to the two-hundred-dollar ticket you gave me? Did you forget something? Maybe you want to humiliate me more? I already admitted to speeding, and you insisted on being a jerk and—"

He held out her license, like right there, and she stopped talking, staring at the plastic in horror, wishing she could go back ten seconds and say nothing. "Forgot to give this back to you," he cut in.

She didn't have to look over to Carol to know she was enjoying this. Daria had to clear her throat, feeling her face heat. Her glasses had slipped down her nose, and she pushed them back up, feeling Mark once again making a fool of her. She wondered whether he enjoyed yanking the rug out from under her, making her look like an idiot. She reached for the license and ripped it from his hand a little harder than necessary.

"Careless on your part, not giving this back," she said rather sharply. "I could have been in a world of trouble if I was pulled over again. Is this something you do often, keep someone's license?" She knew she was deliberately being a pain in the ass, but there was something about Mark that brought out the worst in her, that made her want—no, *need* to have the last word. Fire burned in her belly again because she wanted to argue, refusing to go quietly into the night so he could forget this moment.

He rested his hands on his belt, his heavy gaze lingering intently. "You're quite the firecracker, aren't you?"

What the fuck? Even the way he'd said it, it seemed as if he were toying with her.

"Well, as interesting as this is, I think I'll leave you two." Carol tapped the books on the cart beside her. Her expression was teasing as she said, "Daria, I presume I won't have to bail you out of jail for work tomorrow?"

Daria made herself look away from the arrogance staring her down. "Well, I don't know. Mark, will she?" She just couldn't stop herself.

He didn't pull his gaze from her. Damn, she'd forgotten how vividly blue his eyes were, how they were filled with a spark of mischief that completely rattled her. "As long as she behaves herself, I'm sure she'll be fine," he said, turning from her to Carol, who had evidently picked up on the tension that sizzled between them. Something about the way her boss shook her head and the amused grin that pulled at her lips told Daria she would be grilled well tomorrow.

"I'll lock up on my way out, and you two can finish this little…" Carol gestured, then lifted her hand in a wave as she walked away. There was another second of silence before Daria heard the click of the lock, refusing to look at Mark.

When she did, she had to press her lips together as she pulled in a breath. Her heart was pounding. All the flirtatiousness and fight that had been there a moment earlier was gone. He was so damn alpha, and maleness oozed from his gaze. She forced herself to walk around the counter and reach for her purse, pull out her wallet, and slip the license in. The silence only ramped up the tension.

"So I wanted to apologize."

She hadn't expected that. She flicked her gaze up to him as she set her wallet on the counter and reminded herself to pull it together.

"Okay, so you apologized. For what, again?" For the sex and forgetting her or for being an asshole cop?

His lips quirked as if he were fighting the urge to smile. "For overreacting today, I guess, and for not remembering your name. It was not cool on my part." There it was, that smile that had sucked her in the first time. "And I wanted to see if maybe you'd let me take you out for a drink."

She didn't think she'd heard him right, and she blinked. He was calm and cool, but Daria made herself take a minute as she rested her hand on the counter, feeling as if the rug had been yanked from under her yet again. "Let me get this straight: You came here to apologize for forgetting my name, even though, might I add, it was only two months ago, fun for you and a mistake for me."

He frowned and raised his brows, thinking.

She leaned in. "Come to think of it, you not remembering me at all doesn't say good things about you. I told myself it wasn't about me, but it's kind of like a punch in the face to be so forgettable. But let's just skip right past that and go to the part where you were a dick today in general, giving me a ticket in the next category up just because you could and you felt like it. Now you want to take me for a drink as your way of apologizing for all of this? Or is this a condition to, what, get you to rip up the ticket?"

It was priceless, his expression She could see the second he realized this wasn't going his way. What had he expected, another chance to talk her into the back seat? Some sex, as if she were that easy? And then he would rip the ticket up as if he were some fucking hero?

Yeah, being stupid twice wasn't her thing.

She thought he swore under his breath, his smile now gone. "I'm not an asshole. You having a drink with me would have nothing to do with the ticket. So is that a no? Just say it if it is. I don't need the rant and all the drama."

She realized he actually thought he could walk right in there, toss her that easy smile, and expect her to say yes. "No, not in this lifetime, not ever again. Is that clear enough for you?" she said, walking around the counter to unlock the door and hold it open until he left, when she would lock it behind him. She held her head high and was damn proud of herself.

"Okay then, forget the drink," he said. "Let's just skip right to the sex."

She froze mid-step before turning around slowly, feeling her jaw slacken, and she took in his mischievous grin. Was he serious?

"I'm teasing." He reached out and rested a hand on her shoulder. "I just wanted to see your reaction." Then he pulled his hand away, winked, and said, "Take care, Daria. Oh, and the ticket? Sorry about that, but you're going to have to pay it."

"Hey there, stranger. Haven't seen you in a while. How's life treating you?" said Henry Lewis, the bartender at the Horned Toad, as he settled a pint of lager in front of Mark where he stood at the bar. Henry was tall, light haired, and at least five years his senior. The place was packed with a few familiar faces and a lot of unfamiliar ones, and he couldn't quite make out the music playing in the background.

"Life's good. Can't complain, really," Mark said. "Got a job over in Skagit County as a deputy with the sheriff's department, so been kind of busy." He almost lifted his hand to gesture to his badge, but he was no longer in uniform but a deep blue shirt and faded blue jeans, which was maybe why he felt so damn awkward. He lifted the mug instead and took a swallow of beer.

Henry wiped the counter in front of him and gave a practiced smile. "That's fantastic. Was wondering what happened to you, considering all the time you spent in here, and then suddenly you were just gone, almost like you fell off the face of the earth."

Right, he'd been drinking, picking up women, and doing his best to drown his hurt. Then there was Daria. Wasn't it here that he'd picked her up? He was having trouble remembering. He dragged his hand over his face.

"Excuse me, can I have a glass of white wine, pinot grigio?" a woman called out at the other end of the bar. Henry made his way over, and Mark watched as Daria slid onto a stool beside three other women, wearing a short skirt, boots that went to her knees, and no glasses. He just leaned against the bar and took in her expression—watchful, confident. She was cute, changed from the librarian with glasses he'd gone two rounds with earlier to a casual, attractive woman. Henry settled a glass of wine in front of her, and she lifted it and took a drink. It took him another second to realize she wasn't with anyone, as the three women on the other side of her paid her no mind. Daria lifted the glass, looked straight ahead, and took another swallow.

Now how in the hell could he have forgotten about her? Mark slipped off his stool and reached for his beer, then started walking her way, one step and then another over to the empty stool beside her. He set his beer down as she took another swallow of wine, and her eyes widened as she looked up at him. She wasn't happy to see him, but damn, did she clean up nice, with makeup and mascara, a smoky look that added an allure he hadn't expected. Her hair hung long and loose with waves he wanted to reach out and touch. He wondered about this transformation from nice to naughty, or so it seemed.

"Certainly didn't expect to see you here, looking the way you do," he said.

Daria squeezed the stem of her wine glass between her fingers before lifting it to take another sip. Then she put it down and turned toward him again with what he sensed was a pissed-off vibe. "What's wrong with the way I look?" she said. "You know what? Don't answer that. Or is it that because I'm a woman, I shouldn't be here, having a drink?"

The way she'd said it, he wasn't sure how or whether to answer. It seemed he was walking right into one of those loaded questions. Her gaze flickered with fire, and there was nothing friendly for him in those blue eyes, which offered no give, not for him.

"You just don't seem the type to frequent bars, is all I'm trying to say. Don't take it the wrong way. I mean, I'm just saying, you being a librarian and all, I guess I couldn't picture it. But here you are." He allowed his gaze to slide down over her nice, rounded breasts under a silky tank, slim waist under a short black and purple skirt, and long and slender legs. No, this definitely wasn't Cindy. And this also wasn't Daria, the librarian he'd met earlier. How the hell could he have forgotten her?

"So what you're saying is that being a librarian means I can't stop into a bar for a glass of wine, that I'm supposed to, what, go to a teahouse? Are you saying being a librarian means frumpiness and tea and crumpets?"

He was pretty sure she was setting him up, so he continued to lean against the bar. She sat straight on that stool, her leg crossed so her skirt rode up on her thigh. The hint of skin hidden under her sheer black stockings was just enough to tease him, and he had to force himself to look away when she cleared her throat. Mark lifted his gaze back to hers. Yeah, she had noticed, and she raised a brow. Should he apologize for noticing her fantastic body?

"As I was saying, that's stereotyping and is absolute bullshit," she said. "I don't drink tea. I like going out for a glass of wine, and this is a bar that serves wine. What is it with you guys? Somehow, it's okay for a man to go to a bar alone, but if a woman does it, I suppose you automatically assume she's looking for trouble or to hook up, or she's suddenly free game for some loser. Otherwise, she wouldn't be in a bar. Again, stereotyping, Mark. Don't do it, because people will surprise you. I mean, look at you. I never would've figured you for a deputy. I would've said you were a useless playboy who picks up women." She angled her head, and those blue eyes packed a punch. Her hair was shoulder length, and her earrings were dangly hoops that she wore well. Something about them made her neck appear longer.

He realized she'd just insulted him, but he didn't pull his gaze from her. "Fine, I get it. You're still pissed off. Point taken. So we've both misjudged. How about starting over?" He wasn't sure what she was going to say, as this time she allowed her gaze to slide down over him. It wasn't teasing but deliberate, and it had him wondering whether she was trying to make a point.

"Start over in that you, what, want to get to know me? Or is this another move of yours, saying let's have a drink? I pay for mine, you pay for yours, and then you say, hey, let's get out of here, and then what, more free sex?" She was direct and not quiet.

"Maybe I deserve that, Daria, but my motives are purely to get to know you. That's it, seriously. I'd like to get to know you. What do you say we grab a table? I'll order us another drink, and…"

She said nothing, just leaned on the bar, likely ready to cut him off at the knees.

"I mean it. We'll just talk." Mark lifted both hands in a show of surrender. Damn, why was she being so difficult?

"I don't believe you, because guys like you aren't interested in just talking. You know what, Mark Friessen? I treat people honestly and expect the same." She reached into a small purse on her lap and pulled out a ten, which she tossed on the counter. She swallowed half her glass of wine, then pushed it back and stepped off the stool. "Thank you," she called out to Henry, gesturing sharply to the cash. Henry only nodded, as he was pouring a beer. He gave Mark an odd look.

"What are you doing?" Mark said as he pushed away from the bar, taking in the wine she hadn't finished.

Daria's head just topped his shoulders. She slid her purse over her shoulder and then glanced around as if he'd asked the stupidest question. "I had a drink, Mark. I'm good now. I'm going home," she said. Then she lifted her hand. "Good night."

She turned on him and started walking to the door, and he took in her rounded ass, the skirt, the boots, the tank. She was one hot librarian.

"You're losing your touch, I see," Henry said from behind him as he reached for the ten Daria had left.

Mark took a step back to the bar, lifted his beer, and downed the rest before setting it on the counter. The door had already closed behind Daria. No, he wasn't losing his touch. He was getting his head together, though.

"Do you know who that is?" he said as he glanced back to Henry. He pulled out his wallet and tossed some bills on the counter.

Henry took the money and lifted his gaze, his brown eyes questioning. "No, but I have a feeling you're going to tell me."

Mark felt the smile before it touched his lips. "A challenge, that's who—and one I'm definitely up for."

CHAPTER

SIX

All Daria had wanted was to drink a glass of wine and not be toyed with again by the likes of Mark Friessen. She was digging in her small purse for her keys when she spotted the familiar silver Mustang parked nearby, and she was still trying to understand how she could have let a guy pick her up for a memorable night filled with so much want and regret.

"Daria, wait up."

This couldn't be possible. What the hell did he want now? She shut her eyes a second and then forced herself to turn as Mark jogged up beside her in blue jeans and arrogance. And what did her traitorous heart do but kick up just as her palms started sweating again?

"What do you want?" She knew it had come out quite sharply, but that was what she'd intended.

There it was, that cocky smile. Maybe he got off on women telling him to get lost. Some guys did. "I told you I want to take you out. How about we go for dinner, pizza? Everyone loves pizza. Come on. I know I was a jerk. Don't walk away."

Why was he pushing?

"You don't want to take me out, not really. Seriously, think about it. You screwed me, and I let you, but you couldn't remember my name, and then you couldn't get rid of me fast enough. You never asked for my number, which was a slap in the face. You're a dog, and nothing about you is gentlemanly or even decent, for that matter. For me it was a mistake, and one I don't plan to make a second time. We all have that one thing or two or three that we wish we could undo. For me, it was you. Because I never for one second would have done to you what you did to me." She lifted her brows, and what did he do but laugh?

"Okay, you have me. I'm a dog, but I had a good reason, I thought, at the time," he said. "Boy, I'm making a mess of this. You're right, I was wrong, and I'm sorry. I just…" He stopped talking and gave his head a shake, his brow furrowed. The smile that had lit up his face was now gone. "I'm sorry. I can tell by your face I'm screwing up, jamming my foot in my mouth by trying to explain my reason for doing what I did when it isn't explainable."

"You're telling me you have a good reason for treating me as if I were nothing, just someone of no consequence? You wanted sex. You zeroed in on me, and I took the bait. In fact, I mattered so little you couldn't even take a minute to learn my name or get the hell out of your car and walk me back to mine after you screwed me so intimately in your back seat. Not even one small gesture of caring. Maybe you could've waited a second to see if my car actually started before peeling out and leaving me in the dark to fend for myself. Now you want to, what, have a do-over? You're a disgusting fucking dog."

She fisted her hands and turned to walk away from all that handsomeness that had been her weakness, a pretty face and smooth talking. He seemed to think he was entitled to do anything, have everything, and to hell with any consequences. She wanted to wipe that smug expression right off his face.

"Hey, wait a second." He rested his hand on her bare arm, and her eyes went right there. She stared long and hard at his hand until he lifted it and held both up as if he should've known better. "I want a do-over, but not in how you're thinking. I want a do-over to make things right. Seriously, Daria, give me a chance before I jam my other foot in my mouth. I'm trying to say sorry. You like pizza?" His gaze was direct.

"Sure, of course. Who doesn't?" Why was he pushing so hard?

"Great, so how about I take you out for pizza?" There it was, that confidence. He seemed to think she'd just fall in line, just say yes. She wasn't that easy.

"Like, now?"

He shrugged. "Yeah, I'm hungry and would like to take you out, unless you have other plans."

She could say yes. What did she have to do but go home, where her cat was waiting to be fed and a book was waiting to be read? It was one of the top reads for the week, according to some bestseller list, but she was struggling to get through it. Then there was her flat screen, on which she could binge watch Netflix. She needed to hate him.

"And what if I said I had a boyfriend and have plans already?"

The way he frowned, the way his brow knit and confusion suddenly appeared in his blue eyes, she knew he hadn't expected that. "Do you? Have a boyfriend, I mean." He actually stepped back, and she wasn't sure what his expression meant. It had suddenly and unexpectedly gone from overconfident to doubting. What was he thinking? She should say yes, and then maybe he'd leave her alone.

"No, I don't, but it seems to me as if you automatically assumed I don't have a life. I have a life, I'll have you know —a great life, with lots going on, so much that I have to pick and choose what it is I can do and then say no to the rest." Okay, maybe not so much, but thinking about how little she had going on in her life bored even her to tears.

He just stared at her, and she couldn't put her finger on it, but for a moment she swore he was ready to walk away, or maybe he realized she wasn't worth his trouble. She should let him, so she said nothing else, feeling the awkwardness and the chill from the setting sun, the heat of the day long gone.

"No games, Daria. I've had that. Just a simple yes or no is all I'm asking. I'm done with bullshit from women. Can I take you out for pizza to talk, to get to know you, and most of all to apologize for being an absolute ass? That's all I'm asking."

She hadn't expected his directness and how sharply he spoke to her, all flirting and arrogance gone. He didn't pull his gaze, and he wasn't smiling. She glanced to his Mustang and searched across the busy parking lot for her Sunfire, knowing she needed to walk away, give him just one final "Go fuck yourself," and then he'd leave her alone.

But instead, there was something about the man standing in front of her. He wasn't the man who hadn't really seen her. There was angst, and she thought maybe, beneath the games he'd played, just maybe, there was something real.

He said nothing, and the silence was on her.

"I should have my head examined," she said, "but sure, I'll let you take me for pizza and hear your apology. But that's all, Mark. Pizza, a chat, and nothing else."

There was that smile. "Fair enough," he said, then gestured to his car and took a step toward it. "Shall we?"

She just stared at it, then pulled her keys from her small purse and held them up. "Sure, but how's this? I'll follow you in my own car."

Mark said nothing, glancing off to the side and then back to her, smile gone again. "Okay, boundaries. Got it. Which car are you?"

Of course, he didn't remember. "The Sunfire you pulled me over in," she said before taking one step away and then another.

"Hey, Daria," he called out.

She turned back to him just as she approached her car, wondering what the hell this was.

"We're going to Chippy's," he said. "I'll meet you there." Then he lifted his hand, walked over to his sports car, pulled open the door, and climbed in. And all Daria could wonder was what she was getting herself into, because guys like Mark Friessen didn't have anything to do with girls like her.

SEVEN

Daria slid into a dark brown vinyl booth and glanced out the window to see her car parked in front, right beside Mark Friessen's silver Mustang. She couldn't shake the feeling that he seemed unusually nervous. He lifted his hand to their waitress, a dark-haired curvy woman by the name of Libby, who tossed an easy smile his way. Daria made herself look away, trying to remember the last time she had been in the busy family pizza place in the center of town. It was always packed and had a welcoming vibe.

The vinyl rustled as Mark slid in across from her, and she forced herself to look at a man she knew barely yet intimately well. He reached for the menu, tucked in between the sugar and salt and pepper, at the same time she did.

"Any preference?" he asked. She pulled her gaze from the menu and took in how blue his eyes were. He didn't smile, and he seemed to be considering something.

"For…?" she said.

Mark gestured to her menu. "For pizza. Just please

don't be one of those vegetarians who can't stand to be around someone who eats meat, or if you are, let's at least do half meat, half veggie."

He was talking about pizza. Why was her head jumping to everything else? "Nope, not vegetarian, and I'm not choosy on the toppings. How about the house special? That looks like it has just about everything on it."

"Perfect." He lifted his hand, and the same waitress, who had eyes for him, hurried over.

"Yes, are you both ready?" She glanced once to Daria and then over to Mark, smiling.

"Could we get a large house special, regular crust, and a Coke for me? Daria?" He gestured to her. This was so different from the night he'd picked her up. At least he was now using her name.

Daria flicked her gaze over to him. "Uh, same."

"Okay, I'll get the order in and get you your drinks," the waitress said.

Daria closed up the menu, unsettled. He hadn't ordered a beer, maybe because he really did want to just talk. He reached for both menus and smiled at the waitress as he handed them to her, then settled all of his amazing, powerful gaze back on Daria. It seemed he was more relaxed. A complicated man, he was. The deputy's uniform was hot, but when he was dressed casually in jeans and a simple shirt, like now, she thought he could pull off anything. Damn, why had she thought this was a good idea?

"So here we are," she said, then let out a breath, and he glanced over his shoulder, taking in the room, before settling his gaze back on her. "You have me here now, just like you wanted, out for pizza, as you said, to talk and apologize. So what is it you'd like to talk about? To be honest, how things were left between us, I'm surprised you'd want to make the effort."

It was the silence that always got to her and had her saying the first thing that popped into her head. She wasn't sure if she should be insulted by the amusement that pulled at his lips. But then, what did she really want to say? *Get to the point, and please don't let this be just another move to get me to sleep with you.*

"Don't remember this side of you from our night together," he said. "You're putting me on the spot."

"You screwed me. As I recall, there wasn't a whole lot of talking."

His brow knit, and the amusement was gone. "Point taken. Evidently, I don't know you at all. So tell me about you, Daria. What makes you tick? What made you decide on becoming a librarian? I can tell you right now, you don't fit the image of it. I mean, look at you. You look fantastic, but I have to say, the difference between the librarian and this, it's no wonder I didn't recognize you."

She didn't miss the appreciation for her in his gaze. He clearly meant the makeup, the skirt, the boots, the sexy but conservative look she often went with. "This is me," she said. "I love books, everything about them, so I kind of fell into my job, which requires me not dressing this way for work. Can you imagine walking into a library and seeing this, me, as the librarian? Have to tell you, folks here and the library association aren't ready for it. I'd never have been given the job to begin with, let alone kept it. I'd have been frowned on. I suppose everyone eventually would come around, maybe, but unfortunately, society isn't quite ready for this. So tell me, Mark, what is your image of a librarian, anyway? Would you be one of many citizens here who wouldn't have tolerated me?"

Two could play this game.

The waitress returned with two Cokes over ice, with straws sticking out, and this time, Mark didn't pull his gaze from her. She wondered what he was thinking. Daria nodded to the waitress and even offered her a smile, then looked back at Mark. It was unsettling, to say the least, the way he looked at her long and hard as if he could see under every stitch of clothing she had on. Maybe he was remembering her naked, but then, she really hadn't been. She'd removed only what was needed for a quick fuck in the back seat. She really needed to get that out of her mind.

"I don't know," he said. "Old, gray haired, with thick glasses, wearing sweaters and skirts that a grandmother would wear, practical shoes…" He shook his head, a teasing spark in his eyes. "You've changed my impression for sure. You're not dowdy by any means. And no, I'd never run you out of town for being who you are."

There it was, that smile. She had to fight the urge to fidget. She lowered her gaze to her Coke and then lifted it, pulled out the straw, and took a swallow. It didn't help. She could feel him watching her still.

"You said you had a reason for picking me up and talking me into your back seat, then forgetting all about me," she said. "I guess I'd like to hear it, because it kind of hurts, Mark, that after something so intimate, you didn't even see me."

He pulled his hand across his jaw, and she heard the scrape of whiskers. They were so light with his red hair and gave him a sexy, dangerous look. He was so damn good looking that she wondered why he was with her. He was beyond attractive, extremely hot, giving off an alpha vibe most guys just couldn't pull off. She couldn't allow her head to go any further down that road, though, because this man was a love them and leave them type of guy.

"I had been dating this girl, Cindy. I really cared for her. Loved her." He tapped the table as if to make a point. "There, I'll say it. In fact, I thought she was it. You know, there was just something about her that got right in here"—he tapped his chest—"and that's not a place I let just anyone in. Everything she wanted, needed, loved, I did for her." He gestured with his thumb to the window. "Even that damn car was for her. She loved Mustangs, so what did I do? I bought a damn Mustang."

She couldn't believe they were talking about another woman, let alone one who had led around the attractive, arrogant man who'd used her.

"We shared everything," he said. "She was so hot and excited me in ways I'd never thought were possible. I could see a future with her that I never had before. It was magical, and she sparked these ideas of what I could do and be. Then there was the sex…" The way he was talking about her, Daria could tell he was being pulled into those thoughts, as if reliving them, as he leaned back in the booth. He was clearly still all about this girl. Oh man, this should really be her wakeup call to get up, walk out of there, and not look back.

She squeezed her glass, feeling the icy chill.

Mark shook his head, his expression darkening as he leaned forward, resting both forearms on the table. He stirred his glass with the straw. "And then she fucked me over. I found out that she'd been sleeping with my best friend the entire time I'd been dating her. It was a knife in my back that I don't think I'll ever be able to forget."

Love and hate, she thought. Those two emotions were so close, loving someone one day, hating their guts the next. She could relate, and she realized he had been emotionally fucked over, and he was still taken.

"Ouch, that's bad." Daria leaned back, relaxing a bit,

wondering where the hell this was going yet already knowing.

He rested his arm over the seat back again, fidgeting, tapping his fingers against it. "Yeah, it sucks, being the last to know. I guess that's what really hurt more than anything. Everyone knew except me, and worse, no one said anything. It seemed as if the joke was on me. I don't know how many people said to me, 'Well, how couldn't you know?' or 'Seriously, dude, she was doing it right under your nose, and you didn't see it? We all saw it. Like, what, did you have your head buried in the sand?' or my favorite, 'It was painful watching, and I wanted to tell you, but then I thought it was best to stay out of it and mind my own business.' Like, what the fuck is that? Who does that to someone? I mean, how is it that people would think it was best to just ignore it and not tell me I was being stepped out on, screwed over, and cheated on?"

There was such passion in the way he spoke, but that passion was for another woman, and she still didn't understand what this had to do with her. "You know, that's pretty bad," she said, "and you're right that someone knowing and not saying anything is awful. I can't imagine how I'd feel, but at the same time, I'm not sure how this has anything to do with what happened between you and me. It in no way explains what you keep referring to as your 'good reason' to do what you did to me." She had used air quotes. The awkwardness was back. "Or is this your way of explaining that because you were hurt, I was inconsequential?"

He wasn't smiling. He pulled his hand over his jaw, looking away, over to the waitress. Was he ready to make an excuse and get the hell out of there? "I was hurt and trying to get her out of my system," he said, "so I started dating other women and sleeping with them. No, of course you're not inconsequential. But I can tell by the way you're looking at me that I'm just not explaining myself very well, I guess."

She spotted the waitress walking their way, carrying a large pizza. "You are explaining yourself, but let me just clarify what I think you're saying. The girl you were dating broke your heart, was screwing around on you with your best friend—who is a total shitdog, by the way, because friends don't do that to friends. But nevertheless, back to you and how you were hurt, reeling from being fucked over when you found out. In typical guy fashion, you changed your shirt, hit the bar, picked up a girl to get Cindy out of your system…"

His expression had her stomach knotting. He let out a rough breath as he furrowed his brow, and the waitress settled the pizza on the table between them with two plates. Daria forced a practiced smile up at her.

"Here is your house special. Can I get you two anything else?"

Mark only shook his head. Gone was the flirty smile. "No, that's all," he said, and he waited for the waitress to leave before settling those blue eyes back on Daria. What was it about his eyes? They oozed with something she knew had the potential to crush her. Mark Friessen was not the kind of guy who was in her best interests in any way. She found herself resting both fisted hands on the table, leaning in a bit.

"Maybe I had it wrong," she said. "Something about your face and that timely interruption tells me I wasn't your only pickup. Listening to you go on about this girl, even I can hear she's not out of your system, and you still have your head so far up her ass. How many, Mark? I presume I'm one of many faceless, nameless women used by you. Was I the first, or am I somewhere in the middle? Do you even know?"

She breathed in the aroma of the pizza. Mark had gone still. Sometimes, she didn't like being right. "Wow, really? You don't even know where I fit in. You know, Mark, I'm speaking for all of us women. We have feelings, real, honest to goodness feelings. I'm a living, breathing human being. I bleed, I hurt, I love…"

"I know that," Mark cut in, leaning in. She'd found the very raw nerve he was trying to hide. He glanced to the side, maybe because of how sharply his words had come out. "But at the time, I wasn't thinking of you or…" He gestured vaguely.

"All the other women," she said. "Damn, and you can't remember their names, faces, nothing." Daria let out a sigh, wondering again why she was there. "So, including me, how many were there? You know, how many women did you pick up and screw? All the meaningless sex… I guess I'll never understand how guys can just do that, how it could be meaningless to you. Not that I'm a saint in this, because I was a willing participant, but you forgot my name, my face. Did you screw all of us in the back of that Mustang?"

She lifted a piece of the steaming pizza and settled it on her plate, then realized Mark was still watching her. Those amazing blue eyes appeared confused and ready to argue—or could it be he wasn't happy she'd just called him out? How could she explain to him that he was an absolute dog?

"You want to know how many women I picked up and had sex with? You really want to know the specifics of whether I screwed them in the back seat, or the front seat, or maybe on the hood?"

She had taken a bite, and she just stared in horror as she chewed.

He reached for a piece and tossed it on his plate. "No idea," he said. "More than ten. Fifteen, twenty. I don't know for sure. I didn't keep count. Is that what you wanted to hear?"

She was holding her pizza, and she swallowed, stuck on the number. Like, who did that? Apparently, Mark Friessen and guys who were nursing a broken heart. "No wonder you didn't remember me," she said. "Let me ask you this. Do you remember any of the women, like any at all, even one name? Come on, you have to remember one. Like her over there, our waitress, you screw her too?"

Mark stilled and didn't look over to the young lady who smiled his way again, the waitress named Libby. The horror in his eyes said everything.

"You have no idea if she's one of them?"

He just shrugged. "Do you want me to lie?" he said. He had no shame, or was this how he managed to sleep at night?

"No, I don't want you to lie, but you're being arrogant. I don't even know what to say other than to ask why I'm here, then. Is this a pity thing? Do you feel bad in some way because I called you out for what you couldn't remember?"

He pulled in a breath, then took a bite of his pizza and wiped his hands on a napkin. She wondered whether he was thinking of what to say. "The truth?"

The knot in her stomach tightened. "Please, dear God," she said, "since I don't think it could get much worse after everything you've said."

He'd taken another large bite and let his gaze linger on her as he chewed, confident, arrogant, and something else that said she needed to be careful. "There's something about you," he said.

"Mark! Hey, wow, how are you?"

Daria turned to take in the short woman who was standing there, smiling, staring at Mark and then her, with a man behind her.

"What is this, like, twice in the same week?" the woman said.

Mark dropped his pizza on his plate and leaned back. The tension simmered as he stared at the woman, who flicked her long dark hair over her shoulder. She was wearing blue jeans and a white tank top, with a generous bust, smiling brightly with that happy look some women naturally had. The man behind her was tall, dark-haired, and Daria realized his hand was resting on the woman's shoulder possessively. The way he was staring at Mark and the way Mark stared back at him, she couldn't shake the feeling there was history, and not in a good way. Mark said nothing, and the woman was now looking at her, not just looking but intrusively taking in everything about her with a wide smile.

"So nice to see you out with someone, Mark. Hello, I'm Cindy. Mark and I go way back. I don't think I've seen you around or with Mark before. What is your name?"

Daria couldn't believe Cindy had held out her hand, settling her gaze on her as if she were giving her approval. Like, what the hell?

"Daria." She didn't hold out her hand at first, just reached for a napkin from the dispenser and wiped her fingers, because this was way too weird. Then she did, because it was weirder still trying to ignore her. The girl wasn't going away. Why wasn't Mark saying anything? She looked over to him, and the way he was staring up at the guy, she felt his anger, resentment, or maybe hate. She wondered who would be willing to throw the first punch, because it was clear these two guys weren't about talking anything out.

"Oh, so nice to meet you, Daria," Cindy said. "So you and Mark…?" She let it hang, and Daria pulled her hand away, taking in the happiness on this chick's face. She couldn't get past how forward she was, the familiarity. She had the sinking feeling she was suddenly in the middle of something she had no intention of being in.

"Daria is a friend, a good friend," Mark said finally, likely because of the confusion she knew had to be written all over her face. All Daria could do was once again force a smile, something she didn't do. She wished she could just slip out of there, because Mark was now staring at the chick, again with that lost puppy look. There it was, the gut punch, the reason she was forgettable. So this was the heartbreaker, and this guy was his former best friend? She'd have bet everything on it. It was there in the chemistry, the anger, every heated emotion that only ramped the tension up. She stared at Cindy and wondered what it was about her that had Mark so blind to what she was about.

"Oh, I'm so glad you're getting out again, Mark," Cindy said. "I was just telling Randy that you were looking so down before, and yay! Here you are, out with such a pretty girl. You have no idea how happy that makes me."

Daria wiped her hands again and took in the angst across from her. She wanted to groan and be anywhere but there. What was wrong with him? Couldn't he see she was messing with him?

"So you're the mysterious Cindy," Daria said, then tossed the napkin on the other side of her plate, "who was cheating on Mark with his best friend the entire time you two were dating?"

Cindy's smile faltered, and the guy behind her, who'd

said nothing, finally dragged his watchful gaze, which had been locked on Mark, over to Daria. She wasn't sure whether he was amused or pissed. She thought the latter but didn't really care at that point.

"Uh…" was all Cindy said.

She didn't look over to Mark, who, she thought, tried to hide a laugh. She felt him watching her, so she glanced once to him, seeing something in those blue eyes that resembled humor and mischief, that spark that had been absent since they sat down.

"Yeah, don't." Daria gestured to Cindy. "Not interested in hearing any spin or excuse or anything. It's not my business. This would be a great time for you two to just walk away and enjoy your dinner."

Cindy, whose smile was now gone, looked over to Mark. For what, exactly? Daria wondered whether she expected Mark to speak up and defend her, but all she said was, "Well, we'll leave you to your pizza. This really is one of the best places." Then she smiled as if she hadn't just been called out. She even reached down to Mark's arm, which was now resting on the table, and gave it an intimate friendly rub.

Mark stared at Cindy's hand on him, saying nothing. Then she pulled it away, and ex-girlfriend and best friend were walking off, and then they were gone. Daria didn't watch to see what table they walked to, instead taking in the way Mark lifted a brow as if amused at her. At the same time, she could see how uncomfortable he was, but she doubted in any way that it was worse than how she was feeling, being dragged into the middle of his drama and meeting the princess at the root of all this.

"Well, Daria, you certainly have a way of cutting right through the bullshit," he said. "Didn't see that coming."

What could she say? "And you, Mark, are still in love

with a woman you'll never have. Word of advice? She's messing with you, and she still wants you. That so-called best friend is ready to kill you over a woman who knows how to play the game, and neither of you can see it."

From the way he flinched, the expression on his face, she knew he was ready to argue. "You're way off base," he said. "She's married and has a kid on the way. You're misreading it. She was just trying to be nice." He leaned back and reached for another piece of pizza.

"No, I don't think so, Mark. There was nothing nice about that. She was jealous you were with another woman. If she wanted to be nice, she'd have kept walking, not stopped and said something. Instead, she's dumping salt in your wound because she wants you to keep pining for her. You don't want to believe it, that's your choice. I'm just saying how it is. She wants you, maybe both of you, or maybe she realizes she made a mistake and you were the better choice. It happens. Some women do that.

"While I don't know her, I'm pretty good at reading people. What it all comes down to is that she's fucked up, and she's leading you around, so you're angry, and in turn, you're picking up a slew of women and using them all to ease your hurt." She gestured rather sharply.

Mark shoved the pizza in his mouth and chewed, but as Daria took in the pizza still on her plate, her appetite was gone.

"You know what, Mark?" she said. "I think I'm going to call it a night. This isn't my mess, my problem, but I suddenly feel as if I'm in the middle of a soap opera I have no intention of being in. You've apologized, so you can check that off your list, even though it really was the most pathetic apology. Actually, it was more of you making excuses instead of taking responsibility. Anyway, I forgive you. You don't need to make it up to me. I give you a pass." She wiped her hands again, taking in the remaining pizza. It really had tasted good. Then she picked up her purse beside her to slide out of the booth.

"Hey, wait. Where are you going?" He actually laughed, staring at her with his blue eyes as if she'd lost her mind, as if he couldn't believe she was leaving.

But she made herself stand up and smoothed her short skirt. "Home, where I should have gone before. Enjoy the pizza, Mark, because I like myself too much to get dragged into the middle of something as hinky and toxic as this. You have a thing for your ex. Word of advice? Before you take out or pick up another woman, do all of womankind a favor and end it with Cindy first." She tapped her forehead lightly with her fingers. "End it up here, because three's a crowd. And just FYI, too, not all women are out to mess with you. There are actually some pretty decent ones out there who don't want to be used, who just want one guy to have an honest relationship with."

She slid her purse strap over her shoulder, and for some reason she couldn't explain, she glanced behind her and spotted Cindy sitting three booths down. The guy with her looked both bored and arrogant, and neither was talking to the other. The way Cindy was staring daggers over at her, she knew without a doubt that woman was gunning for her.

Daria didn't think Cindy loved Mark. She was confused and wanted him only so that no one else could have him.

"Good night," was all she said, and this time, as she walked away, Mark didn't come after her.

CHAPTER

EIGHT

When he wasn't a traffic cop, Mark was parked behind a desk at the sheriff's office all because he was a junior rookie, treated like a secretary, picking up lunch and taking messages, doing nothing of importance. He was still considered too green to be of any use. He hated the feeling that no one would ever take him seriously, and he was at a loss of what to do to prove that he was capable. All the choices he had made were about wanting to be treated with respect, yet it seemed his life was going nowhere he wanted.

Then there was Daria and her mouth, that sexy, hot librarian who'd basically called him out and shoved in his face the one thing he knew wasn't true. It couldn't be true. Cindy didn't want him. Her stopping by their table had nothing to do with that. She was just being nice. He was still pissed over the fact that Daria couldn't let it go and instead had just up and left, climbed in that piece of shit compact, and driven away without even looking back.

"Mark, you're still wallowing, I see," said Margery, the sheriff's dark-haired wife, as she walked over to his desk and dumped two files on it. She was a big woman, tall and plump, in blue jeans and glasses, her short dark hair frizzy as always.

"I'm not wallowing, just bored of being told to stay here when I should be at that robbery. That call was for all hands on deck." He lifted his hands as he leaned back in his old wooden chair, which squeaked.

Margery only shook her head as she gestured to the file. "See these here? These are parking tickets that haven't been paid. You need to follow up on them. There. You're not quite so bored now."

He realized she was serious. Parking tickets! He reached for one of the files and opened it to find the carbon copies of tickets, then lifted his gaze to the empty desks of the three other deputies, who'd hurried out with the sheriff. All the sheriff had said to him was "Stay put."

"You're needed here, young Mark," Margery said. "You heard the sheriff, and besides, those tickets need to be paid or your salary won't be. So start dialing."

Mark took in the old rotary phone on his desk, hating this part of the job he'd been relegated to. "You know these tickets aren't a priority," he said. "Two men are at Segways Market, robbing the place, one with a shotgun, leaving how many injured bystanders?"

Margery was already walking away. "You heard the sheriff," she called out. "They don't need your green ass there to babysit and worry about. And it was only one bystander shot. The sheriff called while you were sitting there, moping, feeling sorry for yourself. It was only a flesh wound, nothing serious. They've defused the situation, and disaster's been averted, so do your part so everyone can get paid."

The door to the station opened, and as Mark turned toward it, he felt Margery's motherly reprimand, wishing at least he had a case to work on, something to sink his teeth into. Then he heard a voice he recognized, and as the door closed, there was the woman he was furious with yet still took his breath away. Her dark hair was long and loose, and she was in a blue blouse. He blinked, wondering what the hell Cindy was doing there. Damn, was she in trouble?

He stood up so fast the chair shot back, slamming the cabinet behind him, and both Margery and Cindy were now staring at him.

"Mark, hey, so nice to see you." Cindy flashed him that smile he'd loved so much. It was the kind of smile that flowed out of her effortlessly and had him wanting—no, needing to be with her. It was a sucker punch. Then the phone started ringing, and Margery had that look on her face that said she wasn't impressed and knew way too much about how screwed up his life was. He took one step and another, hearing the squeak of the old floor as he strode over in his cowboy boots. He had to remind himself Cindy was with his best friend.

"Hey, wow, this is, like, so cool," Cindy said, so dramatic, as she took a step toward him, whispering loudly as if she didn't want anyone to hear, which he found odd now. Margery rolled her eyes upwards as she held the phone to her ear.

"Cindy, what are you doing here?" He stopped at the counter, and her eyes reached out to him and tracked his every move. That had been a constant about her, and what did his traitorous heart do but thump long and loud in his ears?

"Oh, I just wanted to stop in and say hi and see how you are," she said. There it was, the smile. Then she glanced over to Margery and tucked her long hair behind her ears as she leaned in closer. "Listen, do you have time to talk? Like, do you ever get a break?"

He just stared. Then there it was, something. Something was wrong. Her taffy-colored eyes, which were always so flirty, now held something that gave him pause. "You drove all the way out from North Lakewood to see me?" he said. "Is everything okay?"

She shrugged and did that thing with her nose, crinkling the skin at the bridge, that had him wanting to do anything he could to find out what was wrong so he could fix it. She let out a heavy sigh. "Not really. I just want to talk to you. You always could sort through and figure out a problem and know how to fix it, and I just kind of need a friendly ear right now to bounce some things off. With your big strong shoulders, you used to always handle and take care of everything, I don't know, Mark. Maybe I shouldn't have come, but you've always been there for me. Can you take a break, and maybe we could grab a coffee or something?"

The way she lifted those amazing deep taffy eyes up to him, he was still stuck on it sounding like she needed him. This was the one thing he'd hoped for.

"Can't take off right now," he said. "I'm the only one here, but come on back and you can fill me in on what's going on. I can't promise the coffee is any good here." He pushed open the gate and held it for her, and there was that gorgeous smile again, for him.

"Ah, thanks, Mark. Could always count on you, and don't worry about the coffee. I just wanted to talk," she said. She wore a jean skirt, her legs bare. As she walked through the gate, so close to him, she pressed her hand to his chest over his light brown deputy shirt.

He gestured to his desk and the wooden chair beside it. "Here, have a seat." He brushed it off first, as it still had crumbs from the box of donuts that had been passed around first thing that morning.

"Thank you again." Cindy looped her purse over the back of the wooden chair as she sat, and for a second, Mark just stood there before realizing what he was doing: staring! *Right, get it together.* He made himself reach for his chair, still against the cabinet, and the wheels squeaked as he moved it forward and sat down. Her blue shirt, patterned with white flowers, showed only a hint of cleavage but clung to her generous bust. She linked her small hands together and then lifted her gaze. Those taffy eyes shimmered with a spark that had his heart kicking up. Just the way she looked at him, he sometimes swore she'd somehow cast a spell. It wasn't sane to feel this way. He linked his fingers over his belt as he leaned back in his chair.

"You are such a gentleman. You always were, Mark Friessen." She offered him a tight smile and held his gaze. "But running into you again last night, I was reminded of how good we were together. I hesitated about coming here, because I really don't want to screw things up for you. Seeing you with that girl last night… I didn't know you were seeing anyone. She's pretty, cute."

He wasn't sure how to respond. He wondered what the problem was. "Daria is great," he said. The last thing he wanted was to talk about Daria with Cindy, even though Daria was the one who had been popping into his thoughts all morning. Too much time to think was not always a good thing.

"Daria. Right, sorry, forgot her name," she said in a way that had him wondering what this was about. She pulled in a breath. "So how long have you been seeing her?" She looked away for a moment, then back to him, angling her head as if fixated on something.

Mark narrowed his gaze. "Not long, why?"

There it was, the smile. She laughed. "Okay, I'm being

nosy, and maybe I don't have the right to be, but I care about you so much, Mark, and I don't want to see you hurt. This is just me caring, is all. And I really do care."

Was she serious? "Hurt by Daria? You aren't seriously implying Daria might hurt me in any way. That's crazy. She's a nice lady," he said. It was him who was the dog.

"Now, just hear me out, Mark. I know you, maybe better than you know yourself. You're absolutely the best. You're kind and considerate, and I guess I never realized what a good thing I had. Some girls see that and take advantage. Guys like you don't come around every day. You always treated me with respect, and I didn't treat you with any decency, and I'm absolutely ashamed of what I did. I wish I could go back and have a chance to do it right, to make it up to you. I mean, we were so good together, and I screwed things up so badly."

His heart thudded again, and he felt the familiar tightening in his chest. Her hand flattened on his desk, and at the thought of those fingers and the way they had touched him, he couldn't get his tongue to move or his brain to come up with anything that sounded remotely reasonable. This was what he'd prayed for, and here she was.

"I was wrong about Randy," she said, flicking those eyes up to him, and for a moment, he thought he saw vulnerability, which he'd never seen before. "If I could go back and undo my bad choice—and it was a horrible one, I can see it now—I would never have cheated on you. I would have told Randy, after all the times he made a move on me, no. But he caught me in a weak moment, Mark. I'd just lost my job, and you were helping your dad with the horses or something, and you were busy. You couldn't come over when I needed you. I know that was selfish to expect you to drop everything, but Randy was just there. I know that's not an excuse. I thought he was someone he isn't. He isn't you, Mark. No one is you."

It took him a few seconds to realize she'd stopped talking. Did she want him back? Or was she trying to blame him for not being there when he didn't even remember that happening? And what the hell had his best friend been doing there, anyway? He was having a hard time understanding where she was going with all this.

"I see," he said. "Actually, no, I don't. What is this?" Maybe he needed her to spell it out, because right now, he thought this was her wanting to come back to him.

She reached over and settled her hand on his leg, and he dropped his gaze to it. It rested there, and she glanced up at him imploringly. Even her touch did things to him he didn't want now. His body was reacting to her with that same wanting. This was bad. No, this couldn't be happening, not here. He gently lifted her hand from his leg, stood up, and stepped back.

"So what is this, Cindy? I'm pretty sure you're wearing Randy's ring on your finger." He flicked his hand to the wedding set she proudly wore. "You're married to Randy, and I heard too that you're pregnant, yet now you suddenly have second thoughts? What, is the honeymoon over? I'm not sure what this is. You made it clear to me what you thought of me. All the while you were with me, you were with him. You weren't honest, and that kind of two-timing is exactly what I never expected, not from you. You lied right to my face, both you and Randy. For how long were you two carrying on behind my back?"

Her smile faded, and she stood up. She was so short, wearing flat sandals, so different from Daria, who'd walked out on him the night before after predicting this very thing. How could this be happening? He ran his hand over his head, ruffling his short red hair, feeling the old squeaky floor beneath his feet and hoping to all hell Margery wasn't listening.

"You're right, one hundred percent right," Cindy said. "I screwed up, and that's why I'm here, Mark. I've done some things in my life that I'm truly ashamed of. What I did to you…I've lost sleep over it, because it wasn't right. If you hated me forever, I guess I couldn't blame you. But please don't hate me. Please forgive me. Please! I need your forgiveness and your friendship at the very least." She had her hands on his chest and his arms again. How the hell had she done that? It was what she did when she was trying to convince him of something. She was always so touchy-feely, and it always had him softening and going along with her.

He pressed his hands over hers and squeezed. He'd meant to pull her hands off him, but touching her always felt so good, and for a moment, he felt himself being sucked back in. He made himself pull in a breath. *Step back, Mark. Get her hands off you.* He heard the voice in his head as he lifted his hands and took a step back.

Her face always showed everything, her joy, her sadness, her misery, her excitement. As her hands fell away, he mourned the loss of her touch.

"You want my forgiveness? Fine, I forgive you," he said. "But you're still married, and you're carrying his baby. Like, what is wrong with you, Cindy? You can't come in here and say you want a do-over after screwing around on me—or is it that you're now trying to hook up with me and screw around on Randy? You're pregnant. Go home. Work it out with him and leave me out of it. You and I are not doing this."

Margery must have heard, as she lifted her head, and from her sharp gaze, he suspected she'd picked up on something. She'd tell the sheriff, and he didn't want anyone in his business. As he walked around Cindy, he gave Margery his back.

"Okay, maybe I deserved that," Cindy said. "But there's more."

He just stood there, staring at her. "What?" He gestured at her sharply, feeling the frustration. It seemed she wasn't going to walk out of there quietly and leave him be.

"He hurts me." She pulled her lower lip between her teeth and glanced to the side, and for a second, he wasn't sure he'd heard her right.

"What do you mean, he hurts you? Randy? We're talking about Randy, right? Are we talking physically? Did he hit you?"

This time, when she lifted those soulful taffy eyes back to him, he could see the hurt she was trying to hide. "You won't find any bruises," she said. "You won't see them on me." She sighed and pulled her arms over her stomach, and he just stared in horror, wondering what else was coming. "Hurting isn't always a fist or leaving bruises or cuts. Sometimes you just can't see the hurt someone inflicts."

He just stood there, feeling an anger he'd never felt before as he thought of the friend who'd stabbed him in the back. "I think you'd better tell me everything, and don't leave anything out."

She put her arms around his waist and hugged him. "Oh, thank you, Mark. I don't know what I'd do without you."

NINE

Damn, the key was stuck again.

Daria yanked and jiggled the glass commercial door to the library, trying to get it just right so the deadbolt would engage. It was all about finding the perfect spot on a door that was decades past its prime. It was time for a new one, but then, this was the oldest building in the area, and it came with what seemed like an old relic of a door just to give her grief.

"Give me a break!" She yanked and banged on the door.

Just then, a warm hand rested on her shoulder, and she jumped, feeling somebody behind her. She glanced up to see the deputy uniform, the hat, the shades. Mark. Why her?

"Let me," he said with that cocky smile, and she hesitated a second before lifting her hand, leaving the key in the lock, and stepping back off the concrete step. She heard the lock click, and he pulled the keys out and held them out to her.

She felt her jaw tighten, wondering how the hell he'd

made it look so easy. "Thank you," she said. "So what are you doing here? The library's closed." She clutched the keys and took in that handsomeness, those blue eyes hidden behind mirrored shades.

"Was driving by and saw you step out of the library, and next thing I knew, I was parking the car and getting out. You walked out on me last night, leaving me with the pizza. I could have just kept right on driving, but I don't like how we left things. I think you owe me an apology."

What was it about the way he talked? His deep, masculine voice could talk her into anything if she wasn't careful. It took her a second to realize he was serious even though it had taken everything in her to get up and walk out that door when she wanted to do anything but. What she really wanted with Mark was something she knew would never happen when he was so twisted up over a girl who didn't deserve him.

"I'm not apologizing for last night," she said. "I did what any self-respecting woman would and should do. You've got some major shit going on in your life, Mark, and I'm not getting caught up in all that drama. It's like a love triangle gone wrong. You're heading the wrong way down a one-way road, and I'm not coming along for the ride, because I already know how this ends: tragically. I didn't realize until she walked in last night and just had to stop at our table, but I saw how you looked at her. She has you hooked, caught, and she ain't letting go. And you can't see it. Not sure what's worse. I see that wounded puppy-dog look you have even though you might deny it. You're fighting it, but the chemistry is there. Even the guy she's with sees it. He was ready to take you on because of her. I bet if she snapped her fingers and said she wanted you back, you'd go running back to her.

"You'd be hurt and still angry, I can see that, but when

a girl gets inside a guy and a guy gets inside a girl, they're suddenly each other's everything. You've never let her go, and she won't let you go, either. No, she wants both of you. What I saw last night were bad choices in the making, stupid ones, really, things you would never do if you were in your right mind, the kinds of choices you'll look back on in the years to come and wonder what you were thinking. One day, you'll wake up after she's played you one too many times, and you'll see how stupid you were and how you refused to see the toxic, destructive triangle you all have going on. That's what I saw last night, and I'm not getting dragged into that."

She didn't know what the hell he was thinking, as he hadn't taken off those damn shades. His smile was long gone. "Mark, you took me out for pizza and talking. Okay, I'll go with that despite how brief it was. You made your apology, and I understand now why you did what you did, picking me up because you were hurt, destroyed, your heart crushed. I really get it. I can see it. You were doing that stupid guy thing of trying to move on with another girl even though your heart, your head, your soul is still with Cindy. So no, I'm not apologizing for what I said or for walking out. And again, by the way, that girl wants you back," she finished. She wasn't sure what to make of the way he was looking at her. She wished he'd take off those damn shades so she could have some clue.

"I didn't say I wanted her back, though." The way he said it. She picked up on the edge, an undercurrent of anger. "And besides, she's married. She's got a kid on the way. She caught me off guard, is all."

"You think that makes a difference to her?" Daria cut in, so done with the fact that he couldn't see the lie he was caught in. "It doesn't. I saw it last night. Why are we even talking about this again? I don't want this in my life, okay?

I have a great life. Let's just chalk up that evening we had to a bad choice and move on. When you see me in town again, you can just ignore me, and at the library too. You don't even need to say hi. Just ignore me and pretend you don't know my name. I give you permission to do that now, and I'll be forever grateful to not have to listen to anything about the girl who broke your heart and made you pick me up and screw me."

She shrugged. "It was inconsequential, in your thinking, because it's all about you, Mark. I mean, seriously, how would you feel if all I did was talk about the guy who got away? If I went through what you did, I'd be crushed, but I wouldn't be talking your ear off about it or picking up a bunch of guys in a desperate attempt to forget. No, I would be working him out of me, working through the hurt, crying alone, binge-watching some series, eating popcorn, reading a book, something, anything that didn't include hurting someone else. Have you not ever wondered why so many women stay single for so long after they break up with a guy?"

He actually took a step back, and for a second, from his amused expression, she thought he was going to laugh. At her. "No, Daria, I wouldn't want to sit and listen to you talk about another guy. You made your point. And no, I guess I've never considered that about women. Do they really stay single after a break-up? I guess I saw the opposite with—"

"Don't say her name." She flicked her hand sharply in front of him, cutting him off again, but he reached for it, and his touch was warm, his hand large and callused. It had her pulling in a breath as her heartbeat kicked up. The touch lingered a moment, and then he let her hand go.

"I got it. No talking about whatshername. I'd just as soon talk about you, anyway. That's why I stopped," he said. When she went to step back, he grabbed her arm. "Whoa, stairs. I don't want you taking a fall."

He was touching her again, and she was suddenly so rattled, feeling his heat as he held her. She blinked, taking in the edge of the concrete steps, and he let go of her arm again. "Well, thanks for saving me from that ungraceful fate, but…" She needed to get away from him, because he was doing that sexy man thing that would end in her doing something that wasn't good for her.

"So what are you up to right now, Daria?" He pulled off his shades and tucked them in the front of his oh-too-sexy deputy's shirt. There was something about the way he carried himself with that gun, the belt, the badge, the whole uniform, and that perfect body. Why had he needed to stop?

"Me, like right now? I'm going home. I've got a cat to feed, a book to read, and…"

Why was he smiling? And it wasn't just a smile. It was that amused grin that pulled at the corners of his lips. Those damn butterflies were back, pounding her stomach. Why couldn't she think of any reasonable answer that would have him walking away? He was still standing there.

"Have you ever been on a horse?" he said.

"Uh, no, why?"

"Well, I was thinking we tried the bar thing, the pizza thing, and they were both a complete bust. Come out for a ride with me. I have horses at my parents' ranch. I'm pretty good on a horse, and I have a gentle one you can ride. If we hit the trail, there's no way anyone is going to interrupt us. Just you and me, some talking, get to know each other out in nature alone, and you'll see there's nothing better than being on a horse on the trail, leaving the world and all the bullshit behind. It fixes a lot."

She realized he was serious. "I don't ride horses. Never

been on a horse. Although I'm sure you're good, I'm not, and I don't have the slightest urge to even try it."

He nodded and glanced away, and her heart sank. This was it, the goodbye she'd convinced herself she wanted.

"What I don't understand, Mark, is why you keep insisting on fixing this with me, talking to me, instead of just chalking it up as a mistake and moving on." She shook her head and gestured between them. "You just keep pushing. I don't understand you."

He suddenly turned serious. "You don't understand me? Well, I don't understand you, Daria, so that makes two of us. I understand nothing about you, and you surprise the hell out of me, which very few have as of late. There's something about you. I said it before, or maybe I didn't, but I sure thought about it. I can't get you out of my mind. I guess what I'm saying is I really want to get to know you."

She wondered if she'd made a face. "You want to take me out to talk and get to know me?"

He nodded. "Yes."

"As in a date?"

He tilted his head, a quirk of amusement in his lips again. "If you have to put a label on it, then yeah."

She opened her mouth to say something, but she didn't understand what the hell was going on with him or what he was really about. She heard the sigh that passed her lips. Her life wasn't filled with excitement or unexpected events. She'd done that only one time, with Mark, when he'd picked her up in the bar. A weak moment, she told herself, when she'd let him talk her into the back seat. That careless, reckless, wild thing wasn't her, and no one she knew would believe it, anyway. That was the kind of thing Daria didn't do. But damn, there had been something about him that drew her to him like a moth to a flame, and she wondered at what point she'd get burned.

"Is this a trick to hook up with me again?" she said. "Because, looking at you, I think you'd have no trouble walking into a place, getting a girl to latch on to your arm, and then getting her in bed before the night's out. I've done that. It's one of those decisions I wish I could go back and undo." She had to look away, and she made herself pull in another breath, because as she said them, the words just hadn't felt true.

"Okay, how about this?" he said. "I promise you I won't try to talk you into bed again. Now that you've pointed out to me how it felt to be on the other end, to be used, I know and understand that I was being selfish. Even though I didn't deliberately set out to make you feel that way, I promise not to be a selfish jerk again. So is that a no to the horse? How about a movie, dinner, drinks, a drive, or just a walk, then?"

She glanced over her shoulder again, seeing his Mustang parked right there. "Mark Friessen, why are you pushing so hard?"

He let out a rough laugh under his breath, and she thought he swore as he pulled his hand over the back of his neck. Frustrated, maybe? "I told you there's something about you, Daria, that has me wanting to spend time with you and get to know you."

She forced herself to nod. Her heartbeat kicked up as she pulled her arms tighter across her chest, trying to settle herself. "So what you're saying is no sex?"

Again, he laughed roughly and resettled his stance. "This sounds like a trick question to me, like I'm walking into something."

She shrugged. "Not a trick question, Mark. Don't look so worried. What if I say sure, I would be willing to date?

Like, let's just label it that, but I want a caveat that we're exclusive, as in no other women while you're dating me. But at the same time, no strings attached. You don't have to call, stop by, hold my hand, or take me out with you on the town with your friends. By my definition, the only thing I want from this dating thing with you is sex. Exclusively."

She couldn't believe she'd just said that. From the way he stilled, the way he stared at her, she wondered whether he'd heard her. He glanced away for a second as if trying to wrap his head around what she'd said. He started to say something, then shook his head, rested both hands over his duty belt, and nodded.

"Sex, you want just sex?" He looked right at her, flashing those megawatt blue eyes on her intently. Damn, he exuded strength. "Where and when?"

She pulled in another breath, feeling the intensity of his gaze, the heat of how he had zeroed in on her. What the hell was she thinking? "Tonight, but I want ground rules. You bring the condoms, and there's no sleeping over. And I'm serious, this is just sex, but one hundred percent exclusive. Think of it as Mark and Daria's new rules to dating."

Mark stepped right into her space and slid his hand around her jaw, holding her there. He was so damn close she could feel his warm breath, and she could've gotten lost in those blue eyes, so intense, filled with such heat. Then he leaned in and pressed a kiss to her lips, softly, tenderly. He lingered a second before pulling back just a bit, still holding her. He ran the back of his hand over her cheek and then down over her shoulder and the bare skin of her arm, so intimately.

"You have a deal," he said. "I'll be there at eight. Now give me your address."

She sensed the demand and something else, as if the

bullshit was gone and he was showing her who he really was. For a moment, she couldn't shake the feeling that he was about to turn the tables on her. Holy shit, she needed to be careful. "No, seven," she said. "I work early tomorrow. And one more thing."

He cocked his head and let his hand fall away, and he waited.

"No just fucking off," she said. "When one of us is done, we have enough respect to tell each other it's over. No games. No walking out the door with a see-ya and then I never hear from you again."

He just stared down at her, that gaze intense, hard. "I can live with that, but same goes for you, Daria. Just sex, no screwing around behind each other's backs, and when we're done, we talk about it like grown-ups. You know what? It sounds like the perfect arrangement to me."

CHAPTER

TEN

"So where are you off to?" Jed said as he strode across the hardwood floor of the family room. Mark, clutching the keys to his Mustang, had just walked out of his bedroom, on the other side of the bathroom he shared with JD and Chris. Voices came from the kitchen, his mom and JD, he thought.

"Out with a girl, a date. Don't wait up," he said.

A date he still couldn't believe Daria had suggested. He could skip all the hand-holding, sweet-talking, and biding his time and get right to what really mattered: sex! He still wondered if she'd change her mind and realize what she'd suggested. He couldn't help the smile that pulled at his lips. The way his dad was watching him, he wondered whether he had any idea what he was thinking. He hoped not.

"A date. Should I be worried?" Jed said. "Who is this date with?" His dad's dark brown hair was damp, threaded with gray, and it appeared he'd just shaved. He was sock footed, in blue jeans and a clean brown shirt, and he didn't appear interested in moving, as he stood right in front of Mark as if he were still a teenager, needing to check in.

"No one you know, Dad," Mark said as he tucked in his shirt, deep blue and white, and rolled up the sleeves before running his fingers through his still damp red hair.

"I hope you know her name, at least," Jed said.

Mark hadn't expected that from his dad. As he paused, he realized his family knew too much about what he'd been up to.

Chris was talking in the kitchen, and there was laughter from Ally and Sophie, he thought. The house was always hopping, crowded, never a place he could have space.

"Her name is Daria, if you must know," Mark said. "She's a librarian. In fact, I've taken her out before."

He didn't know what to make of the expression on his dad's face, humor or something else at his expense? Mark only shook his head and walked around his dad to the kitchen, seeing his nieces perched on the bar stools at the island, eating cookies. He could smell the chocolate chip and knew JD had just whipped up a batch, so that was what the excitement was about.

"Did I hear you say something about a librarian, Mark?" Diana asked from where she leaned at the island, having taken a bite of a cookie. Ah, shit. Apparently his mom had heard. There was something he hated about everyone listening and knowing his business, once again putting him in the hot seat.

"Mark has a date, and apparently, she's a librarian," his dad said as he reached around Sophie, whose chestnut hair was pulled back in a ponytail. He squeezed her, and she giggled. His parents really loved having their grandkids living under their roof, the extended family he figured would always exist here—parents, kids, grandkids. So much for his older brothers moving on and making a life elsewhere. Except there was something about this life that he just knew didn't include him.

"And you know her?" Chris was leaning against the counter, where JD was scooping cookies onto a plate. Mark thought his brother was looking a lot like a pirate, his long red hair tied back in a ponytail, with a perpetual five-o'clock shadow. JD, his sister-in-law, was thin and gorgeous. Her long brown hair, also tied back, had hints of gold. She always had a smile for everyone, including him.

"Of course I know her," Mark said. "Her name is Daria. She's nice, and it's not the first time I've taken her out." He didn't know why he'd needed to add that again. He really wasn't taking her out, but he wasn't about to talk about what they'd be doing, especially with his nieces sitting right there, listening. Damn, he needed to get the hell out of there.

"Well, that's a first," Chris said, never one to let something go even if Mark was right.

"Daria? Daria McKenzie, from the library, dark hair, glasses…?" JD asked.

Great. He hadn't thought anyone in his family would step into the library, but of course his sisters-in-law would. Maybe his mom and dad had, as well, though he'd bet his bottom dollar Chris never had. His mom and JD exchanged a look. He wasn't sure what it was, disbelief or something else.

"Yeah, that's her. So you know she's great, wonderful, really nice. But I have to go. Don't want to be late." He wanted this talk to end before it went any further down the road of how he was still picking up women and tossing them away. This time it was different. He decided to change the subject. "Oh, and you won't believe who stopped by the sheriff's office today. Cindy."

There it was, the look he hadn't wanted to see again on the faces of his mom, his dad, and Chris. JD only shook her head. Mark didn't bother to look down at his nieces even though he knew they'd heard all about the girl who'd broken his heart.

"She said Randy was hurting her," he said. The silence lingered, and he wished he could go back two seconds and shut his damn mouth.

"Why are you talking to Cindy?" Chris said. Leave it to his brother to sound both pissed and ready to lecture him.

"Did you miss the part about her coming into the sheriff's office to see me?" Mark said. "It wasn't the other way around."

"Yeah, I heard what you said. She just happened to drive to another county, to a sheriff's office that has no jurisdiction here?"

Damn, Chris really had a way of getting under his skin. Tension pulled across his shoulders, and he glanced to his two nieces, who also had questioning expressions.

"Now I wish I'd said nothing," Mark said. "She came to apologize, I guess, after I ran into her when I was out with Daria. She just wanted to…" He stopped talking, because he'd been thrown all day by her sudden appearance and the fact that she'd made it known she wanted him back. It was all he'd ever wanted—until now. What was it about her that had him twisted in such knots? Then there was Randy.

"Let me guess: She wants you back," JD said, then took a bite of a cookie and gestured to him with it still in her hand. Diana rolled her eyes as if she already knew the answer, and Mark felt the knot in his stomach tighten, wondering if his family had heard something somewhere, because how could they know she'd insinuated just that? Even he was having a hard time getting his head around it.

"Now, how would you know that?" he said. "In her defense, she apologized and feels horrible for what she did to me, and you know, she even said Randy got her in a weak moment. I can tell by your faces you're taking it the wrong way. Let's just leave it at the fact that I've forgiven her, and—"

"And nothing, Mark," Jed cut in. "She's married to another man, and she's pregnant. Hands off. Shame on her for running to you. If she's in trouble, she has a sheriff's office in this county she can file a complaint with." His dad always had a way of cutting through the bullshit, and Mark wished he were already on the other side of that door.

"I get that, and I told her so, but maybe she's got herself into a situation," Mark said. "She said Randy's hurting her, and coming to me was all she could think to do. Are you saying she should stay in that—"

"If it's true," Chris cut in quite sharply, talking down to him as if he couldn't figure anything out.

Mark glanced down to his nieces, who were taking it all in. His temper was spiking because he didn't like the fact that they were calling Cindy a liar, a game player…what, exactly? "You're doubting her? Why would she lie about something like that? Seriously, you weren't there."

Chris made a rude noise under his breath before JD elbowed him gently. Whatever look passed between them, he figured they'd evidently had a discussion or two, dissecting his life, his choices, and Cindy.

"No one is saying she lied," his mom said in a rather calm voice. "It's just that Cindy was never honest with you, Mark, and the fact that she's now seeking you out and making nice, trying to get you to rescue her, it might be because she suddenly realized you were the better choice. I don't know. It's the kind of thing where, yeah, there would be questions, but if he's hurting her, she should leave. Either way, she shouldn't be coming to you. Your dad is right. She can pay a visit to the sheriff here and sit down and chat with him. I can honestly tell you, Mark, you said she saw you with Daria, and then she suddenly showed up with this story? I guarantee you her motive is to get you back, and it doesn't sit right, even with me. I hope I'm wrong, but I worry I'm not."

Mark said nothing. He'd offered to file a complaint for her against Randy with the sheriff's department there in North Lakewood, but she had just smiled that smile, which once would have made him do anything for her, and said no. "Look, I'm not that stupid," he said. "This is only about Randy hurting her, not her wanting me back. She can want all she wants. I've moved on."

His mom raised a brow, and his dad stared at him with that fatherly gaze that held too much disbelief. He really needed to end this and get out the door.

"Really, you've moved on?" Diana said. "Before you jump to her defense again, let me ask you this: If you had the opportunity to take her back and she asked to come back to you with everything that happened, with all her lies, with how she cheated on you with your best friend, which doesn't get any lower, could you seriously forgive that and believe she wouldn't turn around at the first opportunity and cheat on you with someone else?"

Everyone was looking his mom's way, and he didn't know what to say. He'd been unsettled since the moment she left, feeling as if she wanted him to move her out from the place she shared with Randy and maybe go head to head with someone who had once been his best friend.

"Not answering?" Diana said. "That's good. Maybe you need to have a heart to heart with yourself, Mark, because I didn't raise you to be a fool." She tapped her forehead.

Chris was nodding in agreement, and his dad had a

way of surveying them all and saying everything with just a look. Damn, he was done with this.

"Mark, you're a catch, and she's screwing with your head," JD said, then covered her mouth. "Oops, sorry. I mean 'messing.'" She winked at the girls, who were watching their uncle, the deputy, being taken down a notch or two. "We watched from the sidelines, and I told Chris way back in the beginning that something was off about her. Did I expect her to do what she was doing?" JD stopped and leaned on the island toward the girls. "Okay, cover your ears, both of you." When the girls did so without taking their eyes off Mark, she continued. "She cheated on you, sleeping with both you and Randy. Even I didn't see that coming, but remember something, Mark: Once a cheater, always a cheater. Then there's Daria, a sweet lady who has never steered me wrong with a book. I like her. Don't mess with her." JD rested her hand on the island and gestured to the girls, who lowered their hands.

"Well, this has been a slice, but I've got to go," Mark said. Yeah, he was so done with being taken down a notch by his family. Next time, he needed to keep his mouth shut.

"Right, your date," Diana said. "Enjoy, but, Mark, listen up. Just a word of advice. When you're dating a woman, do her a favor and make sure it's just the two of you there." His mom tapped her head again. "Get Cindy out of your head. This concern you have for her is admirable, but it's not up to you to handle her problems. If she really is in trouble, she can go to the sheriff here, in the county where she lives, by herself and not try to drag you into something she has no business dragging you into. She made her choice. Ask yourself this: Randy is your friend. Would he really do what she's saying?" His mom gestured to him, and he took in the open question from everyone.

"Just to be clear, Randy isn't my friend," he said. "Do I

think he did it? No idea. If you'd asked me if he could hook up with my girl behind my back the way he did, I would have said hell no. So I don't know that he didn't do it, because the Randy I thought I knew evidently isn't the real Randy."

He wasn't liking the direction this was going. He took in the clock on the wall, realizing he was solely responsible for this entire discussion about Daria, Cindy, and Randy. His happy "about to get lucky" mood had disappeared. Damn, he really needed to get his own place sooner rather than later.

ELEVEN

Daria looked around her small, neat and tidy two-bedroom, one-bathroom home, with a cozy fireplace in the living room and a country kitchen with a small dining area. Her laundry room was in the basement, a concrete dungeon she meant to rectify one day. The place was old and dated, but it was hers.

She put in her contact lenses, because glasses were a mood killer, then added more mascara, blush, and a final touch to the eyeshadow before flicking her hair, which she hadn't bothered straightening. She had to admit she looked really good.

She was still shocked she had suggested a no-strings-attached relationship of only sex. "Seriously, Daria, who are you?" she said to herself in the mirror, taking in the hot babe staring back. Her parents, her friends would be horrified if they ever learned she'd suggested what would've been a dream arrangement for any guy. But they were still exclusive.

It was nearly seven. Damn, he'd be there any minute, and those butterflies were back.

What had she been thinking?

She took in her image, the simple black minidress that zipped up the back, and then heard the purr of an engine and a car door outside. Show time! Too late to back out now.

She stepped out of the bathroom, her feet bare, just as there was a knock at the white wood front door. She glanced once to her long-haired northwestern cat, who jumped off the back of the sofa and wandered into the kitchen, totally uninterested.

Daria's heart thudded as she realized what she'd just set in motion. She rested her hand on the knob and then pulled open the door, taking in the tall, sexy redhead standing there, wearing blue jeans and a nice blue dress shirt. He'd definitely cleaned up. His hand rested on the doorframe, and his gaze was unapologetic as he dragged it down and over her.

"Wow, you look fantastic, and that dress," he said. He angled his head and then stepped closer so she could feel his heat. "Well, aren't you going to invite me in?"

"Of course." Daria stepped back, then closed the door behind him.

He looked around before walking straight into the living room, taking in her cream-colored sofa, deep blue chairs, square coffee table, and flat screen on the wall. "Nice," was all he said, looking over to the photos on the mantel: her with her dad when she was ten, a summer camp out with her parents and cousins, and a wedding where she was a bridesmaid to a friend she'd not spoken to in over a year. The clock read exactly seven.

"You're punctual. Did you want dinner…?" she said. Why the hell was she so nervous?

When he turned her way, there was no smile, no flirty spark in those amazing blue eyes. He dragged his gaze over her again, down to her toes and back up, as she walked over to him. The way he watched her was sensual and indecent and unapologetic, but she hadn't invited him over for polite conversation. She stopped right in front of him, so close that he slid his hand around her, right against him. Her hand went to his chest, and she felt his strength, the hard wall of him. She imagined the perfection.

"No, I ate," he said.

Then he lowered his head and kissed her, his hands on her, pulling her to him, all that hardness pressed into her. His hands were on her ass, pulling her up and closer to him. And damn, could he kiss! She linked her arms around his neck. There was something special about kissing a man who knew how to kiss, and Mark did, running his hands over her.

He pulled back, breaking the kiss, and rested his forehead against hers. Yup, hot and heavy, and she was out of breath. Holy God, this wasn't anything like the backseat romp.

"So you're not hungry?" she asked, and this time he laughed.

"Oh, I'm hungry, all right, but not for food," he replied, then lifted her in his arms unexpectedly. She let out a squeal, looping her arms around his neck again. "I'm here for sex. Your deal, remember? Which way to the bedroom?" He started walking, carrying her effortlessly.

"The end of the hall." She pointed, her bare legs over his arm, his other around her back, holding her so intimately as he carried her right over to her queen-size bed and settled her on the white down duvet. Then he stepped back and reached into his front pocket to pull out what looked like a dozen condom packages, which he dumped on the bedside table.

"My responsibility," he said. "You still want to do this?

Last chance." He pulled off his shirt, not bothering with any buttons. That chest, holy crap—absolutely magnificent, and she had to remind herself to breathe. His solid chest, his defined pecs and abs, and his shoulders appeared more than strong enough to hold a woman and carry the weight of everything.

"I say what I mean, Mark, and mean what I say. Yeah, I still want this."

He moved onto the bed over her as she lay down on her back. Her arms slid around his neck as he leaned in and kissed her again, this time deeper, tasting her, as his hand slid up her bare thigh and under her dress, lifting it over her panty-less butt. Yes, it had been daring, but why bother when they would just be coming off? She felt his smile in the kiss as she ran her hands over his back, feeling the warmth, the strength. He pulled back and reached for her hand.

"Come, get that dress off," he said. Damn, he was strong, as he pulled her up and lifted her dress, pulling it over her head and then tossing it to the floor, leaving her naked. For a second, he said nothing as his gaze lingered on her breasts. She hadn't expected the moment of awkwardness, a shyness she'd never been prone to. She forced herself to lean back and put her hands on the bed, letting him see all of her. Mark leaned down and pulled off his cowboy boots, then unbuckled his jeans and unzipped them, pulling off everything so he too was completely naked.

She just took a second to see all of him: tall, lean. His chest was perfection, and his arms... She took in the strength in the cut of his biceps, triceps, and forearms. Then there was the size of him, ready for her. He ripped open a condom package and covered himself, and then he was on the bed again. It was so predatory, the way he reached for both her wrists and pinned them above her head, holding them a moment as he took his time, seeing all of her. He wasn't shy, and it seemed the awkwardness that had been there was gone. Right, this was what she'd asked for.

He had her, so why pretend this was anything but him fucking her, her fucking him? No emotion, no strings. Her heart was pounding again, and she was sure he could hear it as he traced his hand over the flat of her stomach, over her breasts, and then down over her sex, touching her. She hissed and arched, and then his mouth was on her breasts, teasing one nipple and the other as he touched her. He was taking his time, kissing her everywhere, feeling all of her, when she'd thought he would hurry. This was not what had happened in his back seat, where he'd fucked her hard and fast, then pulled up his jeans and climbed back in the front while she did her best to right herself. There had been no appreciation for her body that night, but Mark was taking his time now.

She realized he was watching her. She took in the blue-eyed devil staring down, and the slow easy grin that pulled at the side of his mouth as he settled between her legs, pressed a kiss to her lips, and slid inside her.

CHAPTER
TWELVE

"Hey, Mark, you mentioned you were looking for a place," said Margery, who wore green khakis that day, holding files in her arms as she stood at his desk. "Heard a one-bedroom suite just came available three blocks over. It's a quiet complex, and they're asking only five hundred. If I were you, I'd head over sooner rather than later before it's snapped up. At that price, it'll go quick." She handed him the post-it with a name and phone number scribbled on it.

He didn't look at it before he pocketed it and said, "Thanks, Margery."

She nodded, then waited a second. For what, exactly? Maybe she'd expected him to be more excited, but what could he say? He was still dreaming of his night with Daria. He'd never imagined how hot the sex could be and how simple she'd made it. Just sex, no strings, and no staying overnight. She was hot and responsive, and he thought of the feel of her under him. The last time, he'd been near comatose as she slid down on him and rode him. Yeah, he'd thought he'd go blind from the marathon. How many times, five? Then, before he could fall asleep and his eyes rolled back in his head from exhaustion, she'd shaken him hard and said, "Hey, don't you dare fall asleep, big guy. Time for you to go. Remember, no sleepovers."

Right.

"I'll call right away," he finally said.

She gave him that motherly look again, said, "You do that," and then walked away to the sheriff's office, where Mark could hear him on the phone. The door was open, and two other senior deputies, Jones and Wheeler, had been walking in and out all morning. The sheriff's office seemed to be a hub of activity. He knew they were neck deep in the robbery, the one he'd been left out of. Then there was the vandalism at the garage, the stabbing outside the bar, and the domestic, yet there Mark was, still sitting at his desk, waiting for something other than parking tickets to be tossed his way.

"Mark!" the sheriff called out. His deep, booming voice echoed, and Mark jumped when he appeared in the doorway. The man was his height but had at least seventy pounds on him, give or take. His graying hair was thick, and with his strong personality, even Mark was smart enough not to get on his bad side.

"Yes, Sheriff," he said as the sheriff walked back into his office without saying anything else. Something else Mark had learned about him on the first day was that he was a damn difficult man to read.

Mark stepped into the large office, taking in the old desk and a table off to the side covered with files and papers. Jones and Wheeler, both ten years his senior, were there, as well. He nodded, but they didn't, and he wasn't sure what to make of the way they both tracked him with their gazes. Apparently, they still saw him as green and useless.

"I need you to head over to Ruth Hendrickson's place. Margery will give you the address. Her cat, Misty, is stuck in a tree again. You need to go and get him down."

He was positive it was Wheeler who laughed behind him, and then so did Jones. He was positive *WTF* had to be written all over his face.

"Uh, this is a joke, right? A cat in a tree?" he said. Maybe this was their way of initiating a newbie.

The sheriff shook his head, keeping a straight face. "Afraid not. Ruth is the mother of the mayor, and her cat's in a tree. Go and get it down."

He wanted to argue and point out this wasn't a police matter. "Isn't this the fire department's job? Can't see how this is a good use of my skills," he said. Damn his mouth! What was wrong with him? Even to his own ears, it sounded like he was whining.

The sheriff settled that hard gaze on him. "Just go and do it."

"We've all done it. Your turn," Jones said from behind him.

Mark turned to the senior deputies, whom he knew nothing about. Jones was on the shorter side, wide in the middle, his dark hair looking as if it needed a trim.

"Just a word of advice," he said. "When you get a hold of the cat, don't let it get at your face. It got Wheeler here good an inch from his eye. It's a scrapper."

Wheeler only shrugged, his light hair just past his ears, with a scar on his chin. Mark knew even less than nothing about him.

The sheriff glanced to Wheeler and then back to Mark, who wondered what it was he saw in the two deputies. "The fire department doesn't rescue cats—and the mayor called us. Just remember, he signs our paychecks. You remember who you work for."

Why did it seem he was hinting at something else? The mayor, the town council, and the politicians were whom the sheriff always seemed to be talking to. So what were his options? Argue, or do as his dad had always said to him and his brothers: Just get the job done.

"Fine, consider the cat down," was all he said, then lingered a second. When no one added anything, he walked out of the office, hearing the laughter behind him. Why did it seem as if he was the butt of their jokes?

Margery held out a piece of paper from her desk at the front as he walked towards her, and he took it from her hands, seeing the address of the mayor's mother. "Now, don't take too long," she said, and he was positive she was hiding her laughter.

Mark only shook his head and walked to the door, pulled it open, and stepped out. As he closed it, he was positive she too was laughing.

MARK STOPPED at the office supply store a few blocks from work, and as he pulled open the commercial glass front door, all eyes were on him, the clerk behind the cash register and the two people in line. What was it about a cop walking in? Everyone stopped what they were doing and just stared as if they were thinking he was about to walk over and question them, as if they were doing something wrong. It was ridiculous. But that was one of the first things he'd learned: When someone was nervous, he needed to look harder, because they were evidently hiding something.

"You have backpacks?" he said.

The clerk was dark haired, not very old. He stared at

Mark and said nothing, then slowly pointed. "At the back of the store, over there."

Mark nodded, thinking of the cat in the tree and how he was so done with being the joke at the station. He walked to the back of the store where the backpacks were and picked up the one on sale, no frills, just one zippered pouch and a sturdy strap, hot pink. *Good God!*

Mark walked up to the till and tossed a twenty on the counter.

"For your kid?" the clerk said.

He could've said yes and let that be the end of it. "No, police business."

The clerk frowned as Mark took the change and waved off the receipt. Then he was out the door and back in his police cruiser, driving to the house of the mayor's mother. That was just another thing he was learning about life as an adult, that some people ranked higher in importance than others. He wondered whether an old woman not related to the mayor would be given the same help, but he already knew the answer.

He pulled up in front of a cute white bungalow on a well-treed street. There was a large oak out front, an old woman in a faded pink housedress, and a man who was balding and portly in a sports coat and mustache standing with her. Right, the mayor, and that had to be his mom.

Mark stepped out of the cruiser and took in the large tree as he unfastened his duty belt, which held his pistol and bullets, his cuffs, and his other gear. He set it on his seat as he reached over to the passenger side to grab the backpack.

"Well, it's about time you got here. I called almost an hour ago," the mayor snapped, walking right toward Mark, his hands fisted at his sides. Was he looking for a fight, or was he just an asshole?

"Came right over as soon as it was passed on to me. So what's the trouble?" Mark said. Of course, he already knew, and he heard the pitiful meow, but he wasn't about to cower under this prick just because he was the mayor.

"Misty got himself stuck in the tree again. I've called him, and he won't come down. He keeps going higher." The old woman was pointing, and the mayor was trying to soothe her again.

The lowest limb of the tree was pretty high. He'd have to pull himself up, but he'd climbed worse, way higher.

"So what are you going to do? How are you going to get him down?" the mayor said.

"I'll get him down, but it may be wise, if he keeps getting stuck, to make him an indoor cat. Some just never figure it out," Mark said.

"He doesn't like to stay in the house," the old woman said.

Mark just took in the mother and son and realized this would be one of those pain-in-the-ass parts of the job, where he had to kiss up to someone who expected more than anyone else. This wasn't what he was made for.

He didn't say anything as he slid the backpack strap over his shoulder and jumped to grab the thick branch, then pulled himself up, digging his boots into the trunk and climbing up one branch at a time, picking the sturdy branches and staying close to the trunk. His mom hadn't been able to keep him out of the trees when he was a kid, and he'd scared her more times than he could count by climbing all the way to the very top. He figured that was the source of the gray in her hair now.

Almost there, another branch, and he could see the gray cat just above his head, walking back and forth and meowing. He stepped up one more thick branch on the other side of the trunk, close to the cat, and brushed his hand over him. Misty purred. He slipped the backpack off his shoulder and unzipped the top, then looped it over one arm and held on to the branch with that arm while he reached for the cat. A quick grasp at the neck, and he'd tucked the cat into the backpack before it could scratch him.

He zipped it up and looped it over his shoulder, hearing the pitiful howl and meow, and then climbed down. Hanging from the last branch, he let go and landed hard on his feet. He wasn't sure what to make of the way the mayor was staring at him quietly.

"Wow, you're not like the other deputies," he said. "Geez, what, are you part cat or something? Took those other guys forever, and I thought they'd fall out or kill Mom's cat. I guess we know who to call from now on when Misty gets stuck. What's your name again?"

He wasn't sure what the mayor's frown meant—interest, surprise? He didn't think he wanted to know, as he unzipped the backpack so the old woman with thick white hair could lift out her cat.

"Oh, thank you so much, young man," she said.

Mark let his gaze settle on the mayor, who was waiting for him to respond. He still held the hot pink backpack, which he figured he'd give to one of the girls.

"My name is Mark Friessen, Deputy Mark Friessen," was all he said over his shoulder as he strode to the car. He opened the door to toss in the backpack before reaching for his belt and putting it back on, knowing the mayor was walking his way.

"Well, Mark, I'll be sure to let the sheriff know what a great job you did," he said, then rested a hand on Mark's shoulder.

All Mark could do as he stared at the mayor's hand was think that there was no way in hell he would ever kiss some guy's ass just because of who he was. So instead of saying thank you or something along those lines, he said nothing.

The mayor let his hand fall away, and Mark climbed in his cruiser, pulled the door closed, and started the car. As he drove off down the tree-lined street, he glanced once in the rearview mirror, wondering why the sheriff was so willing to do the mayor's bidding.

THIRTEEN

As he parked in front of the sheriff's office beside the tan pickup the sheriff used and the two cruisers Jones and Wheeler drove, Mark was unsettled for reasons he couldn't put his finger on. He climbed out, taking in the clouds rolling in. His Mustang was parked off to the side, and something about the car had him wondering what he was thinking. It hadn't been about him but about Cindy.

Mark pulled open the front door, with lettering that read *Sheriff's Office*, with *Skagit County* below it. The paint was faded. He pictured his empty desk and the rotary phone. He'd been on the job for only five days. The floor creaked as he pushed open the inside door, seeing Margery first. She raised her brows, and he glanced at the clock on the wall. He'd been gone less than an hour.

"Well, well, well…"

He heard clapping from Jones and Wheeler and the sheriff, who was standing in his office doorway, not even trying to hide his amusement. Mark glanced over to his desk, seeing a tacky sign taped to his chair: *The Cat Whisperer.*

"Wow, news travels fast," was all he said as he walked over to his desk, ripped the sign down, and tacked it to the front instead. He knew they were trying to get under his skin with their needling, and he wondered if this was how his days would play out, being parked at a desk and rescuing cats.

"You have a fan," the sheriff said. "The mayor's mother thinks you're a superhero, and she can't stop talking about the young deputy who scampered up a tree for her cat—who, by the way, according to the mayor, is sleeping peacefully and not all worked up like he gets after being rescued by those two knuckleheads over there." The sheriff gestured to Jones and Wheeler.

Something about those two didn't sit right with Mark. Maybe their personalities or something? Mark didn't sit, just stood behind his desk.

"Notoriety comes with a cost," the sheriff continued, heading over to him. "The mayor's mother is happy, and so is the mayor, which means you're now on his radar."

Mark wasn't sure what to make of the way the sheriff was looking at him, smile now gone. He had a feeling the sheriff wasn't happy about the call from the mayor. "Oh, and is that a good or bad thing?"

The sheriff said nothing, and Mark wondered if he should have asked. Everyone had gone quiet. Was he suddenly on the sheriff's bad side?

"Wheeler, you spend any time with the kid yet and bring him up to speed on how things run here?" the sheriff said, not looking away from him. Mark had that sinking feeling again. He had hoped this would be his ticket to being the cop he wanted to be and knew he could be.

"The kid's barely got his foot in the door and you want me to waste valuable time training him?" Wheeler said.

The sheriff turned. Margery had shot her husband a significant look that Mark hadn't been able to figure out, one that had him thinking everyone knew what was going on except him. So he said nothing.

"I didn't ask for your feedback," the sheriff said. "You have that call you need to make out at the Hendricksons' farm. Take the kid with you."

Mark wasn't a fool. He could see the displeasure in Wheeler's dark brown eyes and the color that rose in his light complexion.

"You show the kid the ropes so he understands we're a family here, so he's clear on how we work," the sheriff said, then gestured to Mark and let his gaze settle on him again. "You don't let us down, you hear?"

Even he knew it wasn't a question.

"I won't, Sheriff," he made himself say.

Wheeler shook his head and then looked up to the old stained tile ceiling. "Well, come on, kid. I don't have all day," was all he said. He was already walking out the door.

Margery was on the phone again, and the sheriff was headed back to his office. The way Jones was looking at him made Mark wonder what, exactly, the sheriff had meant by "how things work."

MARK HAD his sunglasses on and was sitting in the passenger side of Wheeler's cruiser. Wheeler was quiet, saying only, "I'm driving" and "Talk only when spoken to." That was likely why the silence lingered. Mark took in the trees, the countryside, and wondered what kind of call they were going to. He knew it was a farm, the Hendricksons', but nothing else.

"Seems you can follow simple instructions," Wheeler said. "Let's hope this sticks in that green head of yours. When we get there, I talk and you shut the fuck up and say nothing. You understand?" Wheeler glanced over to him, unsmiling, his dark brown eyes hidden behind his own shades. What the hell was Mark supposed to say, considering he was the newbie and he didn't have a clue what was going on?

"So what, exactly, have we been called out for?"

"Apparently, you're not listening," Wheeler said rather sharply. Mark took in the arrogant deputy. This secrecy thing had him feeling as if he were trespassing on unknown territory.

"Oh, I heard you," Mark said. "Shut up and say nothing. Let you do all the talking. Am I supposed to take notes?"

Damn, he just couldn't help himself.

"You have a lot to learn, kid," Wheeler said. "As the sheriff said, we're a family, and when someone new comes into the family, he needs to fit in. There's always an adjustment period. Sometimes that takes time. When you're a cop in a small department, as we are, everyone needs to be on the same page. With family, you always have each other's backs, no matter what."

Mark wanted to say he got it, as the older deputy glanced at him again and then away. Mark looked out his window as Wheeler pulled down a dirt road, with trees and fencing and a barn in the distance. He understood family; he had a great one. His brothers were a pain in the ass but always had his back. But he sensed this was about something else.

"A cop always has another cop's back," Wheeler said.

"It's our code, because we go into situations where one of us could end up dead if backup isn't there. You, kid, we know nothing about you, and you haven't proved yourself to us." There was an edge to his tone. "You're pretty quiet over there, kid. Hope that means you're listening, because there're no second chances. You always back up your brother, no matter what. You don't argue, and you don't question an order, because trust runs very deep. We're not perfect. Sometimes things get heated out there, and you have a split second to make a choice. Is it always the right one?"

Mark just stared as Wheeler pulled in front of a small older two-story farmhouse. He could hear dogs barking as Wheeler turned off the engine, but the deputy didn't get out, just looked over at Mark.

"Sometimes a cop makes the wrong choice," he said. "It happens. It'll happen to you. But you know what family does, Mark? They back each other up. When you're on the same team, when one makes a mistake, you all fix it. And how you fix it is by making sure your family is taken care of. What you see here on the job, it stays on the job. It stays between us. You got that?"

Out of all that, Mark hadn't missed the warning. He shrugged, knowing now why that off feeling was sitting heavy in his gut. "I understand," he made himself say.

Wheeler smiled as he reached over and slapped Mark on the chest. "Attaboy. Come on, time for you to meet one of our local snitches." He went to step out of the car.

"Snitch? So why are we here?" Mark said as he put his hand on the door and gave it a yank, then stepped out of the vehicle at the same time as Wheeler. He heard music coming from inside and took in the overgrown grass and weeds, a broken wheelbarrow by the door. Wheeler waited for him in front of the vehicle.

"We're here because we were told to come here. This is a local snitch, petty thief, drug dealer, and general nuisance. But for us, he's a wealth of information, like with the robbery the other day. You see, our guy Ray may be bad news, but when we show up asking questions about who, what, where, and why, or looking for the one that got away, he answers. He'll know who was behind it, who to call, and if he gives us any grief like he doesn't want to play ball, well, he knows we have a ton of evidence on him for misdemeanors and could lock him up for a long time."

The farmhouse door squeaked open, revealing a scrawny man with stringy long hair and a mustache, wearing a dirty white tank over ripped blue jeans.

"And he's just going to tell you?" Mark said.

There it was again, Wheeler's smile. "He may need some encouragement. Again, what did I say?"

Mark knew what Wheeler was waiting for him to say. "Shut the fuck up and let you do the talking."

Wheeler nodded. "You may just fit in after all, kid," he said. Then he started walking. "Hey there, Ray! Seems a while since we heard from you. You don't know anything about that robbery yesterday, do you? Because I don't remember you calling me. You know the rules and the reason you're walking around, free."

Mark fell in behind the deputy, glancing right and then left, feeling his gun at his side. Ray gave him the feeling of something that had crawled from the sewer.

"You know I don't know everything that goes on," Ray said. "I heard about it, but that's all."

Wheeler gestured to Ray. "Come on out. Anyone else inside?"

Ray was barefoot and stepped out on the crooked stoop as Wheeler rested his foot on the edge of it. The screen clattered, and music was still playing inside. "No one," he said. "Just me and the dogs."

"You wouldn't be lying to me, would you? Because you know what happens when you do that."

Ray glanced over to Mark and made a face. "Who's this? Fresh blood." The way he said it had Mark resting his hand on the butt of his gun.

"He's no one that concerns you," Wheeler said. "Now, I asked you a question, and so help you, you had better tell me the truth. Because you know I mean what I say." He pulled his sunglasses down. Mark wondered what drugs Ray was on.

"You're going to get me killed," Ray said, then let out a groan, lifted his hands, and linked them behind his head. He spun in a circle.

"Only if you don't tell me the truth," Wheeler said. "I'm waiting, and you know what happens when you make me wait."

Mark didn't know what to think, but he knew saying anything was exactly what he couldn't do right now.

"Fine, but you can't tell them it was me," Ray said. "You have to promise…"

"I don't make those kinds of promises. You know that. The deal is that you be honest and call me first. When I didn't hear from you, well, that had me wondering if good ol' Ray was going back on our deal. You going back on our deal, Ray?"

Mark couldn't pull his gaze from Wheeler. When he did, he saw the emotion in Ray, the way his eyes bugged out with fear. This was not a man Mark would have wanted around anyone in his family.

"No, sir," Ray finally said.

"Good. Then I suggest we step inside and you shut off that music and tell me everything."

Ray let his head fall back and shut his eyes a second, busted, capitulating. Then he nodded and pulled open the rusty, squeaky door before going in ahead of them.

Wheeler held the screen door open and stopped in the doorway to say, "You wait out here. Keep an eye on things. I won't be long."

Then he walked through the door, letting it close behind him, and all Mark could wonder was what the hell Wheeler didn't want him to hear.

FOURTEEN

In the quiet of the library, Daria wondered how many times Mark Friessen had slipped into her thoughts. She stared at her cell phone, seeing his name on the screen, and felt a flutter in her stomach, but instead of pressing the green answer icon, she declined it instead.

"Why are you calling?" she whispered under her breath, feeling too many things from the night before. She was more confused than ever. She hadn't expected him to leave her this unsettled.

As she stared at her cell phone, she realized he'd left a message. She glanced over her shoulder to the back room as she reached for her purse, then hesitated only a second before listening to his message.

"Hey, Daria, it's Mark. Just wanted to see how your day was going." There was silence for a second. "Call me when you get this."

She hesitated, sensing she was being dragged into something that could end up breaking her heart. "No, no, no, Mark, I'm not calling you. This isn't how this works."

She reached for her keys and her sweater, tucked her

cell phone in her purse, and lifted the strap over her shoulder before walking out, taking a last look to make sure everyone was long gone. She stepped outside and shoved the key in the old lock, jiggled it until it clicked in place, and then headed straight for her Sunfire in the back parking lot, where it was the only vehicle left. As she climbed in behind the wheel, her phone started ringing again, and she pulled it from her purse and saw Mark's name on the screen.

"Why? What do you want?" She let out a heavy sigh and shook her head, pressing decline again before tossing her phone on the passenger seat. She felt unsettled as she started her car and backed out, then gave it gas as she pulled out of the parking lot and flicked on the radio. By the time she'd pulled in front of her small house and parked, turning off the engine, she heard a car pull in behind her. She climbed out with her keys in hand and took in the silver Mustang and that too-handsome deputy behind the wheel.

He took his time getting out, and the knot in Daria's stomach tightened. She made herself close her door and pulled a hand over her face.

"I called you a couple times," he said. "Did you not get my message? You didn't call me back." He closed his door and started walking her way.

She pressed her hand to the roof of her car and let out a heavy sigh. "I saw you called," she said.

He stopped, and she wasn't sure what to make of his expression. Smiling, he appeared to have something on his mind. He let his gaze linger on her for a second, then looked away and said, "You look nice."

Nice, was he kidding? She was wearing her dark-rimmed glasses, ultraconservative sleeveless shirt, and capris. Boring, plain, as was expected of a small-town librarian. "Just my workwear," she said. "You know, Mark, I didn't know you were coming over." She couldn't smile.

"What can I say? I called and you didn't answer, so when I was driving past the library and spotted you pulling out, I just found myself following you."

Why was she so rattled? She didn't move, so he did, stepping up to her and resting his hands on her shoulders. He pressed a kiss to her lips, and damn, she hadn't expected that. As he pulled back, he let his hand linger on her bare arm, sliding down, then pulled away.

"I can't shake the feeling you're not happy I'm here," he said.

Was he serious? She made herself pull in a breath. "I didn't expect you to just drop by, because that really doesn't fall into my idea of our arrangement. There are boundaries for a reason."

He stepped back and let out a rough laugh that sounded anything but happy. "Well, maybe I don't really have a clear picture of the rules. I don't understand what the problem is. After last night, I couldn't get you out of my mind, and maybe I hoped you would have called, or I expected you to. Honestly, Daria, after last night and how it was, I really thought it changed things a bit here." He gestured between them.

What was it about his expression, the way he watched her with those amazing blue eyes? "Changed things in what way? And why would you expect me to call? Or is that what you're looking for, Mark, a woman who'll call and call, and you can answer when you want? Someone who'll put her life on hold and wait around until you're good and ready to get back to her? No, I won't be doing that. You can call me."

"I did call, twice," he said. He was so close. The way

he was looking down at her, she had a feeling he knew she'd deliberately avoided his call.

"You know what, Mark? You just dropping by like this, I'm not sure if I'm okay with it. For all you know, I have plans. I have a life."

"You make it sound as if I'm stalking you," he said. "I'm not. I kind of had a shitty day, and maybe I just wanted to talk to you. So do you want me to leave? Is that what you're saying? I can do that."

She sensed the edge, feeling how off he was, and she felt like an idiot. She glanced at his arm and saw a long red scratch. "What happened to your arm?"

He took it in and shrugged. "Tree branch, I guess. Had to rescue a cat."

"Come with me," was all she could get out as she reached for his arm. "Of course I don't want you to go," she made herself say.

He hesitated, then shrugged. He really did look off.

She unlocked her front door as he held the screen door open, and she stepped inside and dropped her purse on the chair by the door. Mark closed the door behind them, and she walked into the kitchen and pulled her small first aid kit from a cupboard and retrieved the bottle of antiseptic. Hearing Mark behind her, she turned to see amusement staring down at her.

"You're not really going to put that on a scratch?"

She wondered if he was about to laugh at her. She flicked on the tap and let the cool water run.

"Because it's just a scratch," he said. "It's fine. I've had worse."

She was so unsettled. She reached for his arm, surprised by how he let her take it. As she eased it under the water, she felt him tense. "Don't be a baby. Just humor me."

It was nasty, the scratch. As he pulled his arm back, she turned off the water and reached for a clean dish towel to pat his arm dry, taking care around the scratch, feeling the way he watched her, leaning against the counter as she unscrewed the antiseptic and squeezed some on the scratch. She glanced up, and it was so damn unnerving, those amazing blue eyes on her. He didn't pull his arm back, and she just couldn't explain her need to fuss over him for a moment.

"I think it's good now," he finally said.

She had to look away because she was so damn unsettled. She focused on screwing the cap back on the antiseptic. "Just so you know, a scratch can be a problem. It's not nothing. Didn't know it's part of a deputy's job to rescue cats. Did you really rescue one from a tree?" She furrowed her brow as she lifted her gaze to him.

A smile tugged his lips as he took in the white cream on his arm. "Yeah, for a little old woman. The cat was almost up to the top."

Damn, his smile was unnerving. She knew it would have her doing things she shouldn't for him, so she made herself step away and walk into her living room. She heard him follow her in the quiet, the floor creaking under his cowboy boots. She took in her long-haired cat, curled up on the back of the sofa on a blanket, sleeping. Daria ran a hand over her.

"Not sure how long it would've lasted if I hadn't climbed up to get it," he said.

She had her back to him and realized he was really working it. She fought the smile that tugged at the corners of her lips, then turned and sat in the easy chair in the corner, kicking off her sandals. Her place was neat and tidy, orderly. That was how she lived. Messiness unsettled her. She watched Mark sit on the loveseat, resting his hand on the back and letting his gaze take in the warm and welcoming room.

"So how did you get the cat down?" she said. She didn't know why she was suddenly hit with a wave of shyness.

"Tucked it in a backpack. Picked one up at the store." He shrugged. "It's the only way to get a cat safely down from a tree. You don't know how they're going to react, especially after being stuck for a while. They panic, so for everyone's safety, you tuck them in a backpack or a sack, something easy, so both you and the cat get down in one piece."

Her glasses slipped. There were times she hated wearing them, so she pulled them off and rested them on the end table beside her. "You surprise me, Mark. I never would've expected for you to stop and do something like that. It says something about you, that you're not quite so selfish. Maybe there is hope for you. I mean, I never took you for the kind of guy who likes cats. But you said you had a rough day."

She leaned forward, taking in the change in him. He winced and glanced away, and she had a feeling this wasn't about the cat.

"You ever have a feeling someone is doing something not quite right behind your back?" He had looked away, but she couldn't pull her gaze from him. Heaviness had settled in the air between them.

"We're not talking about the cat anymore," she said. "Did something happen on the job?"

He pulled his hand over his face. "Nothing I can put my finger on. I received a talking-to about how things work, and I have a feeling it was meant to see where I stand. You know, when a cop goes through a door, he needs to know he has backup from his fellow cops or someone ends up dead. I understand that part, but I just have a feeling the talk was about more than that." Now he was sounding cryptic. She realized he was really struggling with something, and he'd showed up on her doorstep as if needing her as a sounding board.

"I read a lot of books, Mark. I've heard about that blue wall, that you back up a cop no matter what. I can only imagine what it's like to go into something, not knowing what to expect, especially when tensions are high, if you don't know what's on the other side of a door, waiting for you. Did something happen? Because I'm getting the feeling you have questions about the cops you work with."

He was looking right at her, and she didn't know what he was thinking. "That's the problem. I don't know anything about them or the sheriff, either. I can't shake this feeling I'm being tested, but for what, I don't know."

Her heartbeat kicked up, but it wasn't from the talk of his fellow cops; it was from him sharing something so personal, a side of him he was letting her see. "So what are you going to do?"

He was looking right at her cat, his arm still over the back of the loveseat. He shook his head. "Keep my eyes open. It could be nothing. Again, I don't know them, and they don't know me." He was looking at her now.

Daria found herself standing up and walking over to him, and he tracked her every step until she stopped in front of him. "That's the thing about new relationships," she said. "There's a time of just feeling each other out, getting to know each other. I can't imagine doing what you do. I can imagine the trust you would need, though, and that's terrifying."

He wasn't smiling. His gaze was hard, questioning, as he lifted his hand and touched hers, her fingers, looking at them. "Are we still talking about the cops I work with, or is this now about you and me?"

She wondered whether he could hear the way her heart thudded. "Maybe I am talking about you and me. Trust and betrayal are two super-vulnerable emotions I don't like to feel. It's terrifying."

Mark stood up, and he was so damn close. He slid his hand under her chin and then tucked strands of hair behind her ears. "It can be if you let it," he said, not pulling his hand away.

"Well, I'm going to take a shower," she said. She slid her hand over his, then linked their fingers. "Do you want to wash my back?"

She hadn't expected the hint of a smile that pulled at the corners of his lips. His blue eyes lingered on her, and he lifted his hand and pressed the backs of his fingers so gently to her cheek that she leaned into it, feeling the caress.

"Yeah, I do," he said, then leaned down and pressed a kiss to her lips. He let his forehead rest against hers, and Daria leaned into him, feeling something different, something changed between them. "And then you can wash mine," he said as he settled his hands on her cheeks.

She couldn't hide the smile as he kissed her again. When he pulled back and reached for her hand, it was him who led her down the hall to her shower. Damn, she was really in trouble with Mark Friessen.

CHAPTER

FIFTEEN

Daria was too comfortable to move as she settled in beside him, laying her head on his chest and letting his arm linger around her, holding him to her. Damn, he was more comfortable than a pillow. She took in the morning light streaming through the window, his hand tracing circles lightly down her back. She lifted her chin, resting it on his chest, and realized he was watching her. His blue eyes were so vibrant and bright, and the way he really looked at her, she wondered what he could see. She was the one who had broken the rule she'd insisted on.

"Good morning," he said, then stretched, and she took in the way the sheet rested on his waist, showing his amazing abs. She settled her hand on his chest. He blinked, taking in the light of the room, and he didn't smile, didn't say anything. Feeling his passion, she realized there was so much about him that she didn't know.

She pulled in a breath where she lay on her side, naked, beside him, feeling his heat and warmth, skin to skin.

"So you didn't kick me to the curb," he said. "You let me stay the night."

He was right, but what could she say? She had craved the intimacy they shared, the touch and his words, just letting her in a little bit. His hand slid over her cheek, brushing her hair back, and she had to shut her eyes because the moment was so tender, the way he touched her, the way he talked to her, the way he said nothing at all.

"Would you believe I fell asleep?" she said.

The way he was looking at her, really looking at her, scared the hell out of her. "Is that what happened, really?" He wasn't smiling, and she knew honesty was the only way here.

"Maybe I didn't want you to leave."

His foot slid over her leg, his hand on her waist, sliding down and over her, touching her everywhere. She was so damn scared, she realized, of what could be, of opening her heart to something unfamiliar. The way he watched her, she hadn't expected him to give her this piece of himself she sensed he'd closed off because of his hurt.

"It's my day off, and I know the library is closed on Sunday. Come home with me," he said. "To the ranch, my parents' ranch, where all my family lives—my brothers, their wives, my two nieces. You'll love it, and they want to meet you. I want to take you riding, out where no one knows where we are, and just spend the day with you."

Her heart was beating, and she didn't know what to say. This was crossing over into a place she was afraid to go, a place where she could get hurt. Maybe he sensed her hesitancy, as he slid his hand up and over her arm and just caressed her. She leaned on his chest, letting her breast press into him as he slid his hand over her back. She rested both her palms on his chest.

"We barely know each other, Mark. I don't know if

that's a good idea. That's not the kind of relationship we have, remember. We're sleeping together, just sex, and…"

He lifted his arm from around her and sat up, and she moved away and sat up herself, reaching for the sheet and pulling it over her breasts as he climbed from bed and stood in front of it, naked, his red hair a mess, his body incredible. For a moment, she thought he would walk out on her.

"Screw your rules, Daria," he said. "I think they're long gone after last night. You want me to say it? I don't want just sex. I want to be able to talk and share and just be with you."

She heard his passion, saw it in the way he stood, looking down at her.

"And why the hell do you want no strings, anyway?" he said. "Because I can honestly tell you that even though that may be what I thought I wanted, there's no way I want that now. I have feelings for you, real feelings. I'm not a fool, Daria. You have feelings too, and you can't hide them. I know you feel this, whatever this is, too. And I'm done with games. I want honesty and something that's real."

She hadn't expected that. "Are you looking for commitment? Is that what this is? What is it you want from me, Mark?" she said as she held the sheet over her breasts and brushed her hair back. He was still standing there, watching her, burning with passion and fire. This was turning into something she hadn't thought could happen with him.

"This isn't about a commitment or a ring on your finger. I'm being real. Maybe I don't want the surface bullshit of just sex and running out the door. Maybe I want to know what the hell you're thinking about, what makes you tick, or just to be able to talk to you about anything or nothing, just to be with you. Is that too much to ask?"

She sensed his frustration as he made a rude noise and sat at the edge of the bed. He reached for his jeans and shoved his legs in, angry, frustrated, shaking his head with his back to her. He was so close. She lifted her hand, fisted it, and then pressed her palm to his naked back and over his shoulder. He stopped.

She felt the tension he was holding, and he turned to her as she said, "So you said something about wanting to take me to your parents' ranch to meet your family." She leaned against him and pressed a kiss to the warm skin between his shoulder blades. The tension slipped away as he turned on the bed and let his arm slide around her, his gaze lingering. Damn, there was so much depth to him that she'd never expected. He leaned in and pressed a kiss to her nose. She wondered if he was expecting her to say more.

"Okay, maybe I too have feelings, but at the same time, Mark…" She stopped and ran her hand over his naked chest, sitting up and taking in the way he was watching her.

"What, Daria? Come on. Honesty means talking."

She shrugged. "Okay, maybe I want something real, no games. But I don't know if you're ready for that." She had to fight the fear that threatened to choke her, not wanting to open herself to that vulnerability.

"I guess I could say the same thing about you. But one thing you should know about me is that I mean what I say. My word means something. No games, just something real. It doesn't have to have a label. Can't we just see how things settle between us and let it happen?" He ran his hand over her cheek, letting his gaze linger again.

"So no labels, but I'm meeting your family, you're staying over, and we're talking."

Damn, he had an amazing smile. He pulled away the

sheet and lowered her back on the bed as he leaned over her, and she ran her hands over his cheeks, feeling the roughness of his day-old whiskers.

"That sounds more like it," he said. "So what do you say? First morning sex, coffee, and breakfast, and then you can meet my family."

She felt her heart crack open a bit. This was something she'd never expected from Mark, and all she could do was nod as he lowered his head and pressed a kiss to her lips. This time, the closeness between them seemed deeper than it ever had before.

"YOU MIND if I ask you something?" Daria said from the passenger side of his Mustang. She was now in blue jeans and a simple blue tank. She turned her head his way, and he took in her light makeup and the fact that she'd put contact lenses in, transforming herself from the girl who worked in a library to this hottie beside him, riding shotgun in a car he was really having second and third thoughts about. Daria was the kind of woman for whom he hadn't ever expected to feel the kinds of things he was, but he'd realized too that something about putting a label on things had never sat right with him.

"No, ask away," he said. He was still in his deputy's uniform, and he ran his hand over his face, feeling the whiskers and realizing he needed to at least keep a toothbrush and razor at Daria's.

"Why do you still live at your parents' ranch? Your entire family is there. What is it, like, some huge place you can get lost in?"

He glanced over to her before looking back to the road. The traffic light ahead of him turned red, and he pressed the brake and stopped. "No, not a big house—the opposite, really. But there's lots of land. My dad gave both my brothers a piece to build a house on, but neither has done anything. Danny is a lawyer, and Chris is kind of running the horse ranch. Dad always did summer horseback riding trips and was always booked. Chris, Danny, and I always helped out while growing up, and Chris has now kind of taken over much of it. My dad used to teach riding lessons, train horses too, and my mom worked alongside him until recently. Now she's a lawyer full time again. She and Danny have kind of set up a practice and are working together, busy with all the local stuff. Danny and his wife, Evie, live in the loft above the barn in a suite, but Chris and his wife, JD, live in the house. You'll see them all. Yeah, that was why I was looking for a place in Mount Vernon, closer to work. The ranch is home, but there's a point where there are too many of us under one roof."

He thought of the lead for that place to rent that Margery had given him. He still hadn't called. What was he waiting for?

Daria said nothing, but he felt her gaze on him. The light turned green, and he gave the Mustang some gas.

"I didn't know you're moving," she finally said, and he glanced over to see that her expression seemed closed off again. Had he said too much?

"Just moving closer to work, is all. I haven't really pursued it. This is a long way to drive every day."

She only nodded and said nothing else. He didn't know what she was thinking, and that was unsettling. His cell phone started ringing before he could say anything else, and he pressed the button on his steering wheel, hoping it wasn't the sheriff's office calling him, because he'd talked Daria into coming out to the one place he absolutely loved.

"Hello?" he said as they left town and he picked up

speed as he turned onto the highway.

"Oh, Mark, I need your help! He's out of control. Please, he's going to hurt me. He said he was going to kill me!"

He'd have known her voice anywhere. The drama was always off the charts. He heard her panic and something in the background that sounded like pounding and yelling, maybe.

"What?" he said. "Where are you right now? Did you call 911?" He glanced in his rearview mirror and pulled off to the side, letting a pickup speed past. Then he gave the car gas again and glanced over to Daria. Her eyes widened as he crossed the center line and turned around, knowing where Randy and Cindy's place was, a newer part at the edge of town with small starter homes.

"Please, Mark, you're the only one who can help," Cindy said. "I'm in the bathroom, and I've locked the door, but he's trying to break it down, and it's not going to hold. Please, I'm scared. Can you come right now?"

He didn't miss the fear in her voice and gave the car more gas. "On my way, but you need to call 911!"

"No, no, no, that will only make it worse. Mark, I need you!"

This was ridiculous. He glanced over to Daria again, who had pulled out her cell phone, and he wondered if she was reading his mind.

"Call 911, Daria," he said. "What's the address, Cindy?"

Cindy rattled it off over the speaker. At the same time, Daria was on the phone to the 911 operator, reporting the domestic dispute. She relayed the address. Damn, she sounded so confident and calm.

He turned the corner and spotted their house at the end of the road, Randy's pickup out front and kids playing in another front yard. "Okay, I'm just pulling up," he said. "Stay where you are." He hung up and parked, then turned to Daria. "You should stay here."

She rested her hand on his arm. "And you should wait until the cops get here. You're a deputy in another jurisdiction. With your ex-girlfriend and ex-best friend, it seems you'll be the match that could light this powder keg. Hear me on this."

What she was saying made sense, but he couldn't let Randy hurt Cindy. "I'll be back," he said. "Stay here." Then he stepped out of the car and strode up to the house, seeing the closed front door but hearing the yelling from inside.

Mark felt his pistol at his side and reached for the knob, wondering if it was locked, but he turned it and it opened, and he pushed it gently, still hearing the yelling and pounding inside. He stood there, feeling anger, feeling a lot of things, and called out, "Randy, it's Mark! I need you to come out here."

There was silence before he thought he heard Cindy calling for him.

"What the hell do you want? Get out of here!" Randy yelled, pissed off.

"Sorry, no can do, Randy," Mark said. "See, I got a call from Cindy. She thinks you're going to hurt her. The cops are on their way, but I need you right now to come on out here, because you and I, we need to have a talk."

There was silence.

Mark flicked the holster, feeling his gun as he glanced in the open door. "Yeah, you're not going to make this easy, are you?" he said in a low voice. He pushed the door open further with a squeak. "Randy, I'm coming in. Remember, I'm a deputy now, and I have a gun, so whatever you do, don't do anything stupid."

SIXTEEN

Daria couldn't believe Mark had walked right into the house—a house he had no business walking into, because this was the ex-girlfriend who had mastered playing games, and Mark was just one more guy completely blind to whatever her agenda was. She stared, furious, because he was supposed to be smarter than that, and instead, he was running toward a girl he should have been staying far, far away from.

Daria stepped out of the Mustang. The neighbors to the right were shooing their kids into the house, and she heard the sirens closer now. A few neighbors had stepped outside, staring at the open door Mark had just gone through.

She rested her hand on the car door and wondered about the wisdom of standing there. When she closed the door, she heard the yelling from inside and hesitated, taking in the green shrubbery and the small porch.

Two cop cars with lights flashing were pulling up in front, and she stayed where she was as the cops approached. Just then, she heard what sounded like fighting from in the house, the sound of fists, maybe, and a crash as if something had been knocked over. A girl screamed. Daria stared, hearing another loud bang, a wall or a door. Then the front door burst open, and she had to step back, stunned, as Mark brought out Randy.

He was cuffed, and blood dripped from Mark's lip. From his expression, his determination, she could feel Mark's anger. Behind them, Cindy, a woman she'd never forget, raced out of the house barefoot, in sweats and a white tank, her long dark hair hanging loose and tears streaming down her face.

"You jerk!" yelled Randy. "You were screwing my wife! I swear I'll kill you. You come into my house… Get these damn cuffs off me!" He was fighting Mark.

The two cops wrestled Randy as he struggled to pull away. They somehow dragged him to one of the cruisers and stuffed him in the back. He was still yelling, but she couldn't make out what he was saying. She knew her mouth was open. She couldn't believe this shitshow, wanting to say something but having not a clue what.

"Oh, Mark, you came!" Cindy cried, making a beeline for him. "I just knew you'd come. You always come. He's crazy! I told you he was going to kill me."

Daria stared in horror as Cindy threw her arms around his waist, pressing her body against him. He didn't look her way, and she couldn't pull her gaze from them, horrified. Mark rested one hand on her back. What the hell was he doing?

"Ma'am, were you the one who called it in?" one of the deputies asked, moving in front of her. All the while, she was reeling from the gut-punch of watching Mark with another woman.

He said something to Cindy, and she felt her hands fisting. She glanced once more to see his arm around an ex who was fucking with his head, and damn, she wanted to kick herself for being such a fool.

"Yes, I called," she replied. "I was in the car with Mark Friessen over there, and Cindy called him and said her husband was going to hurt her. She wouldn't call the police; she called Mark, who told me to call you, and here we are." She had to fight the urge to look over to him, as she silently reminded herself she wasn't into this drama and would never be the odd woman out. The cop was still standing there. "I can't help you with anything, as I don't know them. I just made the call. Mark told me to. I don't know Cindy or her husband."

She realized Cindy was now talking to the other cop, pulled aside, and Mark was walking her way, wiping the blood from his lip. She just stared at him. The deputy she'd been talking to walked over to him, closing the gap, and said something. She wondered if they knew each other. Mark patted the deputy's arm, and then he was walking her way. Anger simmered in her stomach, her chest, as he stopped in front of her.

"Sorry about that." He glanced over to the car Randy had been stuffed in. Behind him, Cindy was gesturing wildly, out of control, close to losing it. Daria had seen it before, the kind of drama she didn't want or need. There she was again, feeling as if she were being dragged into something against her will all because she'd refused to say no to a man who was no good for her.

"You were hit?" She wanted to touch his lip, which was swelling a bit, but that only angered her more. Why couldn't he see the problem here?

"Yeah, Randy got one off on me. Seems he's got it in his head that I'm back with Cindy."

Daria reminded herself that another scene was exactly what wasn't needed there. She pulled her arms over her chest, wondering why he was so damn dense. "And you don't think it's possible she put that very idea there?" she said.

She hadn't meant to say it and didn't know what to make of the way Mark was watching her now, likely thinking up ways to defend the drama queen. He glanced once over his shoulder and then back to her as she took in a neighborhood she wasn't familiar with.

"Yeah, I figured as much," he said.

She flicked her gaze up to him. She didn't have a clue what to say. She glanced around again and finally said, "Good. I'm glad you figured that much out."

The way Cindy kept looking over, she figured it would be only another second or two before she came up to them and convinced Mark of some other reason she needed him there.

"Just to be clear," she said, "is this where you need to run me home, or maybe I should find my own way, because you're going to be tied up dealing with Cindy and whatever this is?"

She wasn't sure what his expression meant, but for a second, he stilled. His blue eyes narrowed and flickered with what seemed like a warning. "What would ever put that ridiculous idea in your head?" he said. "Why do I need to take you home? Remember, we're going to the ranch so you can meet my parents, my family, or have you suddenly changed your mind again?"

Was he serious? The way he stared at her, she thought he was angry at her.

"Seriously, Mark, we're standing at your girlfriend's house because she still has a thing for you and doesn't want to let you go. She needs to be sure she has you within calling distance. I'm not a fool. I can see it. She called and you drove right over here." She stopped. His expression was that of a man who didn't want to hear what she had to say. She couldn't shake the feeling that he'd always be one call away from running out to save Cindy. There would always be something.

"She's not my girlfriend. You're my girlfriend," he snapped, then rested his hands on his duty belt. Her gaze went right there. She didn't know how to get through to him.

"Mark, you may say that, but actions speak louder than words."

"You're right, Daria, they do. So what the hell are you getting at?" He gestured behind him to where Cindy was staring daggers her way.

"You just ran into a house you had no business going into, and only moments ago she was in your arms, crying, while you comforted her. Mark, she's scared of her husband, yet instead of calling the cops, she called you, and you turned the car around and raced over here to save her."

He shut his eyes, but not before she saw his frustration. "She ran over to me, but maybe you should have watched a little longer and seen when I gently moved her out of my arms. I'm a cop. I've sworn to uphold the law and protect the public, including Cindy. Of course I'm not going to turn my back if she's in trouble. I'm going to come over and do something, even for her, but it doesn't mean I have feelings for her anymore. Daria, haven't you figured it out already? There's something about you that's so fucking real. You're not stringing me along."

She wanted to touch him, but she let her arms fall to her sides and unfisted her hands, trying to understand Mark and what this was. She had to force a swallow past the lump in her throat. "And what about Cindy?"

He stepped closer and brushed back her hair, tucking it

behind her ear. It was a gentle touch, and he didn't look away, as if she had all his attention, and it completely unsettled her. "What about her? There's no Cindy in our equation. She's married. There's only history between us. It's just you and me and the date we have today." He was saying all the right things, so why was she so damn scared?

"But you were so in love with her, so twisted up, and it wasn't that long ago that I could see she was still inside your head." She pressed her hand to his chest.

Mark groaned as he stepped back, and she could see the frustration in those vivid blue eyes before he dragged his hand over his face and fisted it. She thought he swore under his breath before looking back at her. "Let me tell you something about that. Whoever wrote that song 'Thank God for Unanswered Prayers'? Well, all I can say is he really knew what he was talking about when he wrote it, because he was so, so right. And maybe I didn't get it until you. You're right, she had me so twisted up with bullshit and lies, but, Daria, I never expected to feel this way about you, so much so that I'm glad it's you here with me, not her."

He said nothing else, letting his gaze linger. She could feel his angst, his passion, and shut her eyes for a second. It would be so easy to believe him. Maybe he knew, as he was right there, so damn close, sliding his hand over her shoulder and her cheek. She flicked her gaze up, looking into all that handsomeness.

"You're going to need some ice on that," she said, gesturing to his lip, where blood was drying.

He smiled and winced, touching it. "I've had worse. It'll be fine. You're going to have to be a little tender with me for a bit."

She settled into his arms and then rose up on her tiptoes to press a kiss softly to his lips. "Like that?" she teased as she pulled back, feeling his warm breath as he brushed her hair back from her forehead. There was something about the way he touched her.

"Now you're getting it." His eyes lit up, and he slid his hand over her shoulder and said, "Time to go."

He reached for the door of the Mustang and pulled it open, waiting for her to settle in the passenger side before he strode around and climbed behind the wheel. He shoved the key in the ignition, and she listened to the purr of the engine as he pulled away. His ex-girlfriend was sitting on the front step with one of the cops, appearing miserable, not pulling her gaze from Daria and Mark as they drove away. Just something in the way Cindy watched them let Daria know the woman would always have a thing for Mark. She wondered what she'd pull next.

As his hand reached for hers, she dragged her gaze over to meet his. "So, to your parents' ranch?"

He tossed her another easy smile. "Yeah, and no more distractions. My family would love to meet you, Daria. Given any thought to getting on a horse?"

She realized he was serious and acknowledged that there was so much about him she still didn't know. "How about just one major thing at a time, like meeting your family?"

He glanced over to her, and she wondered what he was thinking. "I guess that's all I can ask, then. Family first, and then I'll ease you onto a horse."

She felt the smile on her lips and the joy in her heart. Damn, something about Mark was absolutely perfect. "Sounds like a plan, Deputy Friessen."

Turn the page for a sneak peek of
new crossover series!
NOTHING AS IT SEEMS the first book in the Billy Jo McCabe
Mystery Series
Available in print, eBook and audio

A NEW CROSSOVER SERIES!

The Billy Jo McCabe Mystery

Nothing As It Seems
Hiding in Plain Sight
The Cold Case
The Trap
Above the Law
The Stranger at the Door
The Children
The Last Stand
The Charity
The Sacrifice

The social worker and the cop, an unlikely couple drawn together on a small, secluded Pacific Northwest island where nothing is as it seems. Protecting the innocent comes at a cost, and what seems to be a sleepy, quiet town is anything but.

The Social Worker

Billy Jo McCabe wants only to help children overcome their troubled lives, as she herself struggles to forget the childhood nightmare she survived. She took sociology and prelaw at the insistence of her adoptive father, Chase McCabe, and learned how to use power tools from her adoptive mother, Rose. She loves reading in the backs of bookstores before tucking the book back on the shelf and slipping out without paying. She has a fondness for peanut butter and dill pickle sandwiches, has a three-legged cat named Harley, hates running (because that was all she did as a kid), and secretly binges on brownies and red wine on the sofa in front of her TV every Friday night.

She's never been married and has dated only twice. She visits Chase and Rose when summoned and shows up dutifully for every holiday with her family, but she has no siblings to speak of, and she feels a growing resentment for the mother who abandoned her in foster care. Despite proudly maintaining the same prickly attitude that nearly landed her behind bars as a kid, she has yet to speak up to Chase, who interferes in her life too frequently, ready to fix every problem, whether she wants him to or not.

One thing no one knows about Billy Jo is that she moved to Roche Harbor because it's the only clue she has about the last known whereabouts of the woman who abandoned her.

The Cop

Mark Friessen, son of Jed and Diana Friessen, has landed accidently in the role of small-town detective, a position in which he's going nowhere. Nearly married once, and broken-hearted three times, he's sworn he'll stay single forever, and he keeps his tattoo of a former girlfriend as a reminder that only fools fall in love. He's tall, attractive, and stubborn, and he refuses to live in the shadow of his two older brothers, Chris and Danny.

As Roche Harbor's youngest detective, he sleeps with a gun under his pillow. He has a stray dog that won't leave, and he swears that the only two food groups that exist are meat and potatoes. His favorite drink is black coffee in the morning, sugared coffee in the afternoon, and a shot of whiskey in his coffee at night to keep him warm.

*** *Each book in this series is a complete book, with no cliff-hangers, and can be read as a standalone. However, these books may contain references to situations from earlier books in the series. As with any long book series that focuses on specific characters, their changing relationships, and how their lives continue to unfold, you may find it more enjoyable to read the series in order of publishing, as there will be developments and changes in the relationship dynamics of the core characters.*

NOTHING AS IT SEEMS
A BILLY JO MCCABE MYSTERY, BOOK 1

Protecting the innocent comes at a cost, and what seems to be a sleepy, quiet town is anything but.

"A compelling story that touches on powerful social issues"

— BOOKBUB REVIEWER

NY Times & USA Today bestselling author Lorhainne Eckhart brings you the first book in a new crossover series! The social worker and the cop, an unlikely couple drawn together on a small, secluded Pacific Northwest island where nothing is as it seems.

Billy-Jo McCabe never expected to become a social worker, considering the broken system nearly destroyed her. Shortly after she takes a job on a remote Pacific Northwest island, she gets a call about a missing girl.

Meanwhile Roche Harbor detective Mark Friessen is called in to investigate the disappearance, but instead of working with the newly appointed social worker, he ends up butting heads and clashing with her every step of the way. Billy-Jo becomes the rival he does his best to avoid, considering the only conversations they have involve her pointing out his shortcomings and arrogance.

But when Billy-Jo finds herself in over her head, she's forced to team up with the man who has the uncanny ability to bring out the worst in her and together, they come up against close-mouthed locals, island secrets that hit too close to home, and the realization that their case about finding and helping a young girl has turned into something far more sinister.

NOTHING AS IT SEEMS

CHAPTER 1

"Have you ever seen a more stunning place in all your life?" said the woman leaning beside Billy Jo against the ferry railing. She had a short blond mane, shapely curves, and long, long slender legs, wearing a red skirt and tank top that left little to the imagination.

Billy Jo knew the woman wasn't talking to her.

"Sure," came the reply from her other side, "if you love bad coffee, misbehaving tourists, weekend partiers, over-priced food, general mischief, and trash tossed everywhere on the beach every night and every morning."

What was it about his voice, deep and brooding? She took in the guy. He had on a worn jean jacket, blue jeans, and sunglasses, giving off that bad-boy vibe she knew girls loved.

"Well, that's a negative outlook of such a beautiful place," said the blonde. "Are you visiting or are you a local? Oh, let me guess! You live here."

Billy Jo wondered whether she should step back so she wouldn't be in the middle of this pickup, knowing well that the blonde was working this tall, ruggedly attractive guy. Even she had shamelessly allowed herself to ogle him discreetly from behind her own shades. There was just something about the man who was leaning against the railing—pensive, quiet, brooding. He would likely be first in line to get off the ferry when it finally docked, and she'd be second off this rattling bucket of steel.

This time, the man actually glanced her way. She wondered whether he thought she was going to add something, but she refused to look up from her cell phone after seeing the latest text: *Check in with the chief of police as soon as you get there. He wants to meet you. Oh, and we got a call about a possible situation.*

She took in the grime on the steel deck of the ferry. Beside her were two hardtop suitcases, one large and one smaller, both thankfully on wheels. She could see from her peripheral that the man was watching her shamelessly from where he leaned.

Just then, the horn blasted to announce their approach, which had her jumping and the woman beside her shrieking. She swore under her breath, because what did that good-looking asshole do but laugh at both of them? She wondered if it was at her expense or the blonde's.

She glanced at some litter in the corner, which no one had bothered to clean up, and pulled up the handle of one suitcase. As the ferry jerked, she had to take a step to keep her balance.

"That was so loud," the woman said, actually leaning over to her as if they were the best of friends. "Don't they warn you?"

The hot guy was still laughing under his breath as if this were his daily source of entertainment. His hair was red, striking, short and messy. She knew the girl was flirting, whereas he seemed to be playing that not-interested game. He was tall, attractive, likely with the kind of alpha personality she was quite familiar with.

She wasn't impressed.

She needed to disembark, both from the swaying motion and the fact that apparently, there was a situation she had to check into. She didn't like situations, because they always came with the kinds of questions no one wanted to answer.

"It's a ferry," Billy Jo said. "They're loud and noisy."

And crowded, she thought, as the only way off and on the island. Now she was wondering at the wisdom of taking a job here.

She realized he was looking right at her from where he leaned, and she found herself under his scrutiny, dragging his gaze between her and the blonde. Maybe he was comparing them.

"Let me guess," he said. "You girls are here to do all the tourist stuff and look for a good time, or trouble, or something."

She realized he was including her in his evidently pretty low opinion, and she had to fight the urge to glance over to the blonde. She couldn't do that, though, as she was now pretending to look at her phone, which she held in one hand. Her bulky purse, which held everything else, was tucked over her shoulder. She pulled in a breath to set him straight.

"Oh, we're not together," said the blonde. Of course, she had jumped in. "Nora Cassberger is my name, and I'm on my own—totally, not that it wouldn't be fun hanging with you and everything…" She touched Billy Jo's shoulder, and her gaze went right there to her hand. Seriously?

Just dock the damn ferry, already! This was totally humiliating, and she had things to do, like find out what the hell this mysterious situation was.

The guy pulled down his sunglasses just a bit so she could see the most amazing, brilliant blue eyes. The guy seemed to ooze trouble. She wasn't sure what to make of his unsmiling expression or the way he didn't seem at all embarrassed to stare at her and then the blonde. *Right, Nora.*

Maybe this hadn't been such a great idea, standing at the front of the ferry, in front of the cars, so she could be one of the first off. But she was counting the seconds, and then she'd never have to see this guy again.

She forced herself to give everything to her cell phone and ignore him, because nothing good ever came with a guy who looked like that.

"I don't remember seeing you here before," he said. "You just another visitor, or do you have a reason to be here?"

Was he talking to her? The question seemed more like a demand.

Just then, her phone dinged with a sixth message from her dad, Chase McCabe, about her car, her cat, and the rest of her things, which he would be bringing over himself. She had insisted on moving away, starting a new life in a new place, looking for answers to questions she wasn't about to share with anyone.

She pulled in a breath to answer the jerk, this time powering off her phone and tucking it in her purse. "You know, not that it's any of your business, but…" she started.

He was now looking over at the blonde as if he hadn't been talking to her.

Asshole!

For a moment, she considered stepping back, but the dock was right there, and she would soon be able to get off this damn ferry and out of this awkward situation.

He was leaning on one arm now, looking right at her,

not the blonde. This had to be a joke. Her mud-brown hair was nothing special, and she had freckles over her nose. Her plain face was without makeup, and her capris and dark blue shirt were not only baggy but also comfortable. She wondered if she made a face.

She finally glanced over to Nora just as a gust of wind blew her skirt up, revealing black lace and killer thighs. Nora shrieked, and Billy Jo just shook her head, so glad she hadn't done anything stupid like wear a skirt.

Nora laughed then, and the way he stared—no, ogled, she knew he was just another guy who enjoyed the show. "I guess someone should have warned me about the wind," Nora said.

Billy Jo could feel her jaw slacken as she rolled her eyes. Seriously?

"I'm just here for a little getaway, is all," Nora continued. "Maybe you could recommend something fun, you know, touristy stuff, like great restaurants, nightclubs, anything like that. I mean, where is your favorite place to hang out?"

"Hey, Mark, smoke!" one of the ferry workers shouted to the bad boy beside her, gesturing to a cloud of black smoke wafting up just as the ferry docked.

She found herself looking to where he was pointing, a smaller house on the hill, past the line of cars waiting to get on. She heard him swear under his breath. Just then, there was a *pop-pop-pop*, followed by screams and shrieks.

"Get the ramp down!" Mark yelled.

Pure instinct had her ducking and crouching behind her suitcase. She knew well the sound of a gunshot. Mark moved under the rope. Evidently, he was someone important, and she found herself really looking at him from where she was crouched. The metal gate was still closed, but the ramp was coming down. Mark hopped the metal fence in his cowboy boots and was on the ramp as soon as it was down far enough.

"Keep everyone here until it's clear!" he shouted, jogging up the ramp.

There was a loud boom, followed by another dark cloud of smoke and another *pop-pop-pop*. What the hell? This was supposed to be a safe, quiet island, not some crazy city.

She listened to the shrieks, people ducking and taking cover, though the ferry worker wasn't. Something about his demeanor told her this wasn't anything unusual.

"What do you think happened? Are we under attack?" Nora said, crouched right beside her, almost touching her. She realized the few passengers that had been standing behind her, waiting to walk off, were gone. Apparently, they'd taken cover, whereas she was right out in the open.

"I have no idea," she said.

Another ferry worker appeared, younger, tall, lanky, his pants two sizes too big, with not a care in the world. She could no longer see Mark running. Just who the hell was he? The ramp was now down, and people were in their cars. One of the ferry workers was talking on his radio as he stood in front of the metal gate, holding the latch, the only thing keeping it closed, waiting for…what? Why the hell weren't they concerned?

"Excuse me, what's going on?" Billy Jo called out from where she was still crouched, really questioning what the hell she was walking into on this island. "Is that gunfire, someone shooting?"

"Ah, just CJ Krantz," replied the ferry worker, "one of the old-time locals. Always something going on up there. Has a mess of guns he shoots off when the visitors here get too crazy for him, too noisy, bothering him. He says there are just too many of them here, so he shoots off a few pops in hopes of scaring people away. He's harmless, though."

Harmless… Was he kidding?

She heard a crackle over the worker's vest radio, and she slowly stood up. The smoke was fading, and there had been no more pops. She spotted who she thought was Mark putting out a fire with a hose, then heard a siren as a firetruck pulled up at the house.

The ferry worker lifted his hand and circled it. "All clear! You can unload," he called out to the other worker.

Billy Jo just stared in horror, because she knew well that guns and crazies weren't a good mix. "Whoa, just wait a second. You said this was a local shooting off guns? And is that a fire?" She gestured to the small old house, still seeing smoke from under the water. A few other people were up there now. Nora was holding her arm, and Billy Jo glanced back at her, taking in the spooked look.

The ferry worker just shrugged. "Mark took care of it. Likely a propane tank exploded on the barbecue at the back of the house. It's all under control."

"Wait, but that was gunfire—and who is Mark?" she asked.

The ferry worker pulled open the gate and gestured to her, and she knew to move. "Mark is a detective here on the island. He knows CJ and his shenanigans. He likely had the barbecue too close to the house. He's up there now, so the gun situation is handled. Don't worry, and welcome to Roche Harbor."

Something about the way he said it made her suspect he took some enjoyment in what had happened.

Great. So much for a sleepy, quiet place. She wondered what other surprises she'd be in for. She took a step, pulling on her suitcases, and the blonde fell in beside her.

"That was exciting! And that was a local cop? Wow, do

you think he's single?" Nora said, still talking to her as if they were friends or something.

Billy Jo just stared at her. "I have no idea," she said.

But she did know that guys like that were exactly the kind of trouble she'd made a point of keeping off her radar.

About the Author

"Lorhainne Eckhart is one of my go to authors when I want a guaranteed good book. So many twists and turns, but also so much love and such a strong sense of family."

— (LORA W., REVIEWER)

New York Times & USA Today bestseller Lorhainne Eckhart is best known for writing Raw Relatable Real Romance where "Morals and family are running themes." As one fan calls her, she is the "Queen of the family saga." (aherman) writing "the ups and downs of what goes on within a family but also with some suspense, angst and of course a bit of romance thrown in for good measure."

Follow Lorhainne on Bookbub to receive alerts on New Releases and Sales and join her mailing list at Lorhainne-Eckhart.com for her Monday Blog, all book news, give-aways and FREE reads. With over 120 books, audiobooks, and multiple series published and available at all, retailers now translated into six languages. She is a multiple recipient of the Readers' Favorite Award for Suspense and Romance, and lives in the Pacific Northwest on an island, is the mother of three, her oldest has autism and she is an advocate for never giving up on your dreams.

"Lorhainne Eckhart has this uncanny way of just hitting the spot every time with her books."

— (CAROLINE L., REVIEWER)

The O'Connells: *The O'Connells of Livingston, Montana are not your typical family. A riveting collection of stories surrounding the ups and downs of what goes on within a family but also with some suspense, angst and of course a bit of romance thrown in for good measure. "I thought I loved the Friessens, but I absolutely adore the O'Connell's. Each and every book has different genres of stories, but the one thing in common is how she is able to wrap it around the family, which is the heart of each story." (C. Logue)*

The Friessens: *An emotional big family romance series, the Friessen family siblings find their relationships tested, lay their hearts on the line, and discover lasting love! "Lorhainne Eckhart is one of my go to authors when I want* *a guaranteed good book. So many twists and turns, but also so much love and such a strong sense of family." (Lora W., Reviewer)*

The Parker Sisters: *The Parker Sisters are a close-knit family, and like any other family they have their ups and downs. Eckhart has crafted another intense family drama… "The character development is outstanding, and the emotional investment is high…" (Aherman, Reviewer)*

The McCabe Brothers: *Join the five McCabe siblings on their journeys to the dark and dangerous side of love! An intense, exhilarating collection of romantic thrillers you won't want to miss. — "Eckhart has a new series that is definitely worth the read. The queen of the family saga started this series with a spin-off of her wildly successful Friessen series." From a Readers' Favorite award—winning author and "queen of the family saga" (Aherman)*

Billy Jo McCabe Mystery: *The social worker and the cop, an unlikely couple drawn together on a small, secluded Pacific Northwest island where nothing is as it seems. Protecting the innocent comes at a cost, and what seems to be a sleepy, quiet town is anything but.*

Lorhainne loves to hear from her readers! You can connect with me at:
www.LorhainneEckhart.com
lorhainneeckhart.le@gmail.com

Also by Lorhainne Eckhart

The Outsider Series
The Forgotten Child (Brad and Emily)
A Baby and a Wedding *(An Outsider Series Short)*
Fallen Hero (Andy, Jed, and Diana)
The Search *(An Outsider Series Short)*
The Awakening (Andy and Laura)
Secrets (Jed and Diana)
Runaway (Andy and Laura)
Overdue *(An Outsider Series Short)*
The Unexpected Storm (Neil and Candy)
The Wedding (Neil and Candy)

The Friessens: A New Beginning
The Deadline (Andy and Laura)
The Price to Love (Neil and Candy)
A Different Kind of Love (Brad and Emily)
A Vow of Love, A Friessen Family Christmas

The Friessens
The Reunion
The Bloodline (Andy & Laura)
The Promise (Diana & Jed)
The Business Plan (Neil & Candy)
The Decision (Brad & Emily)
First Love (Katy)
Family First
Leave the Light On
In the Moment
In the Family

In the Silence
In the Charm
Unexpected Consequences
It Was Always You
The First Time I Saw You
Welcome to My Arms
Welcome to Boston
I'll Always Love You
Ground Rules
A Reason to Breathe
You Are My Everything
Anything For You
The Homecoming
Stay Away From My Daughter
The Bad Boy
A Place of Our Own
The Visitor
All About Devon
Long Past Dawn
How to Heal a Heart
Keep Me In Your Heart

The O'Connells

The Neighbor
The Third Call
The Secret Husband
The Quiet Day
The Commitment
The Missing Father
The Hometown Hero
Justice
The Family Secret
The Fallen O'Connell
The Return of the O'Connells

And The She Was Gone
The Stalker
The O'Connell Family Christmas
The Girl Next Door
Broken Promises
The Gatekeeper
The Hunted

The McCabe Brothers
Don't Stop Me (Vic)
Don't Catch Me (Chase)
Don't Run From Me (Aaron)
Don't Hide From Me (Luc)
Don't Leave Me (Claudia)
Out of Time

A Billy Jo McCabe Mystery
Nothing As it Seems
Hiding in Plain Sight
The Cold Case
The Trap
Above the Law
The Stranger at the Door
The Children
The Last Stand
The Charity
The Sacrifice

The Street Fighter
Finding Home

The Wilde Brothers
The One (Joe and Margaret)
The Honeymoon, A Wilde Brothers Short

Friendly Fire (Logan and Julia)
Not Quite Married, A Wilde Brothers Short
A Matter of Trust (Ben and Carrie)
The Reckoning, A Wilde Brothers Christmas
Traded (Jake)
Unforgiven (Samuel)
The Holiday Bride

Married in Montana

His Promise
Love's Promise
A Promise of Forever

The Parker Sisters

Thrill of the Chase
The Dating Game
Play Hard to Get
What We Can't Have
Go Your Own Way
A June Wedding

Kate & Walker

One Night
Edge of Night
Last Night

Walk the Right Road Series

The Choice
Lost and Found
Merkaba
Bounty
Blown Away: The Final Chapter
He Came Back

www.ingramcontent.com/pod-product-compliance
Lightning Source LLC
Chambersburg PA
CBHW031001210726
48290CB00007B/2411